House of God

Eric David Ami

ANUCI PRESS

HOUSE OF GOD

House of God

A Novella

Everything that lies ahead belongs to you and me.

Well, the moon is broken, and the sky is cracked
Come on up to the house
The only things that you can see is all that you lack
Come on up to the house
~ Tom Waits

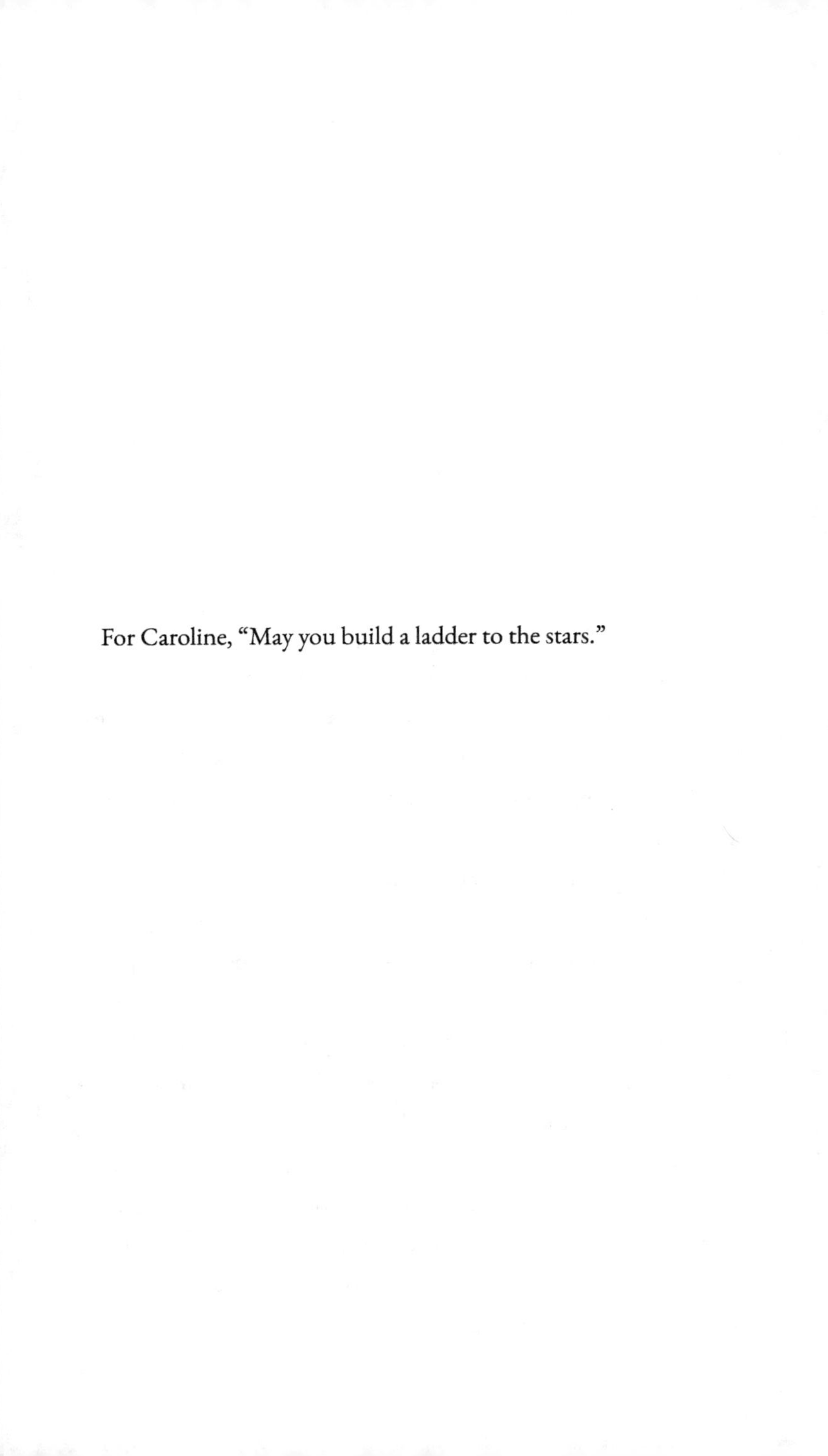

For Caroline, "May you build a ladder to the stars."

$$\mathcal{O}ne$$

You wake from a deep sleep, the kind that makes you question if you really did sleep or if you were just lying there suspended in the great unknown. Your phone vibrates and chirps from the kitchen, where you left it to charge. You hope the buzzing will pass, but it doesn't. It repeats like a threat.

Groaning, you look over at your wife. You are not married, but at the age of 33, you despise the term girlfriend. "Wife" is easier. She lies there in a deep sleep with your four-month-old daughter. You envy them.

As silently as you can, you get up and shuffle across the bedroom while praising the apartment for being carpeted. Pushing open the door, you slip into the darkness of the hallway.

As you enter the small kitchen, the phone charging on the counter illuminates the room in a fading umbrella of white light. You reach down and grab the cell phone to silence the buzzing. As you do so, you see a series of missed calls and four texts. Your stomach drops, and your chest tightens as you read the messages.

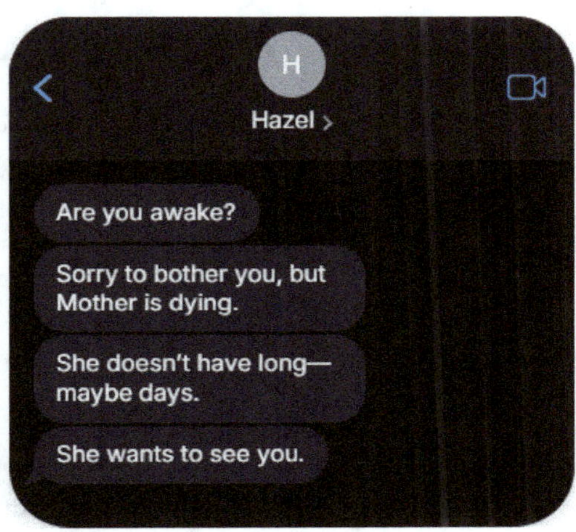

The darkness that fills the rest of the apartment crawls toward you. You squint and do not blink as the words scratch into your brain.

Mother.

Dying.

See you.

For some reason, a Bob Dylan song passes through your mind. You mutter the opening lines as you open the fridge and grab a series of beers. You power off your phone and leave it on the kitchen counter. With a few short steps, you exit the kitchen and enter the living room. With a grunt, you sit on the sofa that you hate. It takes three beers and ten minutes before you fall into a dream.

***

From the corner of a basement room, we look down upon YOU, six years old, wrapped in a thin white blanket and sleeping on a metal cot. A thick pipe, maybe water, runs the length of the cold, dark, vinyl-tiled room. It's clear that this isn't a bedroom but instead a storage or utility room, but it's a room nonetheless.

The silence is like thunder as we slowly move in toward you. Just as the frame of the door is about to disappear, we see that it slowly cracks open. More darkness spills inside. And with it, a figure in white linen crawls, claws inside on all fours like some sort of crustacean.

We push in towards your face. Your eyes are closed tight with fear. We do not see anything, but instead, we hear the sound of sniffing. At first, it's faint, but it grows louder as the figure gets closer to your face.

From the corner of our perspective, an unknown face covered with long black hair appears to inhale you. It's seemingly drinking in your scent. You feel and smell the hot breath, maybe coffee, smothering your face. The moisture builds around your quaking eyelids.

The intruder lingers for centuries. Just as the atmosphere becomes unbearable, we slowly pull back to the corner of the room. As we do, the white linen figure scuttles out of the room. The door clicks shut. You do not move. Eventually, you fall into a version of sleep you do not like.

The sound of your baby cooing, the clink and clash of pots and pans, and the high-pitched cartoon voices coming from your television wake you. Your eyes are heavy with cheap beer, and your mouth is sandpaper. You are grateful to be here, and then you remember your phone, the message, and the request.

Looking down, you see that the cans of beer are gone. You look up and see Nayeli watching you as she beats the hell out of a bowl of eggs.

"What happened, huh? Why did you do this?"

Rubbing your eyes, you get up, kiss your bouncy, high-chaired daughter, and sit on the kitchen table that you hate more than the sofa.

"Why'd we have to get such a tall table, Naye?"

"Don't you change the subject," she says as she pours the defeated eggs into the pan that your ex-girlfriend bought.

The room is filled with the comforting sound of sizzling breakfast. You draw in the smell as you rest your chin in your hand.

"My sister blew up my phone last night."

Nayeli moves around the kitchen like a dancer. In one hand, she has a knife, and in the other, she has your phone.

"What do you mean, blew up?" she says as she tosses your phone at you. You barely catch it.

"It's a figure of speech," you say as you push your tongue against your teeth to hide your irritation at her inability to understand pointless and dumb phrases.

"You hate your sister so much you drank all the beer, huh?" She shakes her head as she minces cilantro and onion like a surgeon.

"Hate and dislike are different."

"What did she want, tell me?"

You can tell she doesn't really care but rather wants to fight. You take a second to think about whether you should drop a line of sarcasm, but the idea is too exhausting in your current state.

"Said my mother is dying, and she wants to see me."

The sizzling changes its tune as the onion hits the ham you didn't know was in the mix.

Naye looks at you with a soft nod. "Breakfast will be ready soon. Go shower."

***

You love hot showers: the feeling of water scalding your body, the drowning of hangovers, and the emergence of unfiltered thoughts. It's your think tank. The apartment complex charges you for the water, but some things are worth the cost.

***

Back at the dining room table, you feed your daughter smashed avocado and egg. 90.09 FM plays Joao Gilberto. The patio sliding door is ajar, and a stray autumn breeze fills the room.

"You know I'm Mexican, right? This is Brazilian music." Nayeli says this in her trying-to-be-funny voice.

"I don't control what they put on the radio. And I thought you were Filipino?"

Your banter is always like this – always on the knife's edge of a fight. It's stressful, but it's the only way you can get through the day.

"So what are you going to do?" Nayeli asks you curtly. She has this extraordinary talent that makes you feel like you're inconveniencing her.

"About my dying mother?"

"Yes."

"I'll have to deal with it, I guess," you say. The mere idea of the situation has made you weary – the kind of tired your body gets when it's missing essential vitamins.

"She caused you so much pain, fuck her," she says sharply.

"Don't curse in front of the baby, come on."

Nayeli waves your comment away, "I don't understand you. That woman isn't your mother. Your mother is supposed to take care of you—"

"Oh, like your mother?" you say sharply.

"I had my mom for twelve years. They were good years, loving years – years that I would not trade. Your mother just shat you out and let you survive."

A boiling rage starts from your stomach and rises to your chest. You breathe it down and try not to take her insensitivity to heart. You know that, despite her crass and shattered glass words, she is ultimately correct.

"When my dad died, he left me with unanswered questions, do you understand? I can't live with more...not from her. I need to see this through. I need answers, closure."

"Be careful what you wish for. You may not like what you hear."

Her words, full of truth, echo in your head as you finish feeding your daughter. You take a few sips of coffee and a couple of bites of egg before pushing yourself away from the table and declaring that you are going to pack a bag.

"I'll be back tomorrow."

You wait for a minute, but she doesn't say anything. She just eats her eggs and chorizo. Turning, you head back into the bedroom to pack.

The bedroom holds a soft morning light that comes from the ancient aluminum windows that look down at the apartment pool.

You take a moment and enjoy the Zen of the now. It brings you a sort of calm. There is something about the way the sunlight hits the wall that stirs a certain lost nostalgia hidden inside you. But the thought is fleeting because the weight of your reality draws you back to your story.

You start pulling your pants, shirts, socks, and underwear from the dresser, and you think about what lies ahead. It's not the three-hour trip into the Illinois country in a car that's pushing 180K miles or the inconvenience of your mother's death that occupies your mind's eye...

<u>In your mind's eye:</u>

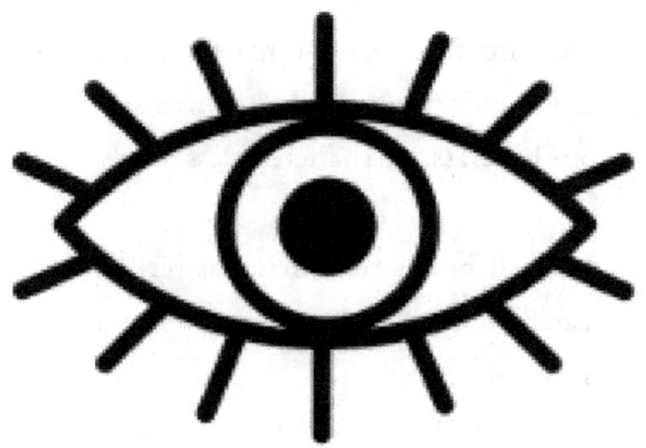

The thoughts in your head are massive trees drenched in darkness. The trees are so close together they seem to be touching.

As you stare at them, rooted as much as they are, a dense sighing pushes through the dark leaves above. You cannot see through the canopy. It's an ocean of rolling blackness. The sighing travels down and through the wall of trees that loom ahead of you like ancient sentries. They open up to reveal the sprawling house behind them.

Your vision focuses like a camera. All that you see is the black, dirty, decaying Carver House – an unholy monolith rotting like an infected tooth jutting from the sorrow-drenched soil. Everything is full of lies, screams, and perversions. The house, now superimposed against a tar-black background, begins to breathe: exhale and inhale, exhale and inhale, exhale and inhale. A pair of arms slip around your waist and tear you from this waking nightmare image.

You are grateful to Nayeli for bringing you back. Her hands rub your stomach and slowly make their way to your waist and under your waistband; she has you in her soft, always-lotioned hands. She begins to slowly rub and squeeze you. It doesn't take long for you to fill her hand and more. You turn around and kiss her deeply. She takes off her nightgown and pushes you on the bed. With ease, she pulls your pants off and slides on top of you. A picture on the nightstand falls to the floor, and silently, passionately, she tells you without speaking that she loves you.

***

A hundred miles later, you can still feel Nayeli on your fingertips as you drive through the gray October afternoon. In vain, you try to focus on the fleeting memory as the roads melt from city highway to backcountry interstate faster than you expected. Cold yellow cornfields, decrepit barns, and lonely houses pepper the scenery. Everything is far away.

The melancholic landscape, with its stretch of empty plains and lonely skies, brings to mind the cold, cold desolation of Kansas in *Capote*, a fantastic film that is more than just an account of a writer's life – in its own way, it's a story about loneliness, and about a great many things, things that you know too well, things that perhaps you have known longer than you would care to admit, such as writing itself. It was some time ago that you discovered in a quiet, fleeting moment of youth, the small, faint ability to write a story – unique stories that you wanted to read that carried with them some weight, or at least you thought, and yet, once shared with a circle of certain cynics, those words, your words, were met with strong chortles and scorns that rendered you naked. It did not take long for you to bury the pen and pick up a hammer, thinking, perhaps, or at least lying to yourself that the hammer weighed more in purpose. Now, writing, the very thought of it, is that cold, cold Kansas or even a splinter lodged deep in your finger. A splinter that, over time, has burrowed its way in so confidently that it can never truly be removed, and though fresh skin has grown over it, making it forever a part of you, you still feel it daily, sometimes more than once, as you run your finger over it, checking, as if by performing this ritual, it will give you access to the shattered idea. Or you simply do it to make sure it is still there.

The phone rings. It's your half-sister – Sister Hazel. (She is called this because of her eyes and her love for the band). It takes a second wave of ringing for you to answer it.

"Yeah," you say.

"Are you driving?" she asks.

"Yes."

"She doesn't have long."

"I know. I read your text."

Beat.

"The others, they may come."

The buzzing of the phone and the friction from your uneven tires occupy the silence. You let it linger for a moment.

"I didn't think about the others."

"I know, that's why I'm telling you."

"You should have told me before."

Beat.

"Would you have not come?" she asks faintly.

"Does it matter?"

"Mother is dying."

"I know."

Beat.

"I...we miss you."

Your stomach writhes and burns as if an eel is passing over an ulcer. You feel sick. Rhythmic, heavy, wooly breathing comes through the speaker. You shutter and terminate the call.

The radio, which was humming nothing but static, starts playing Eddie Noack's "Psycho." The way he says "Mamma" starts to hurt. It's the kind of hurt that comes with fear. But you're not sure if it's fear from the pain coming, or the pain from the past.

Your ears pound even though the volume hasn't been touched. You slap the radio off, pull off the interstate, and grind onto Route 12, also called Talbot Rd. It doesn't matter to you what the crumbled road is called because it leads to the place you'd rather not be.

A half mile later, ahead and to the right, a large faded sign looms in front of a gas station – once a symbol of hope when headed out, but now, as you approach, it carries with it a choking dread, the faded letters in highway gothic font little more than ancient ruins that do not bid you welcome. When headed in, it reads:

Welcome to Carver.

Diamond-speck raindrops fall on your windshield as you drive past the specter of a sign and into the small gas station parking lot without turning on your wiper blades. You sit for a long moment, counting the plop, plop, plops of rain hitting your car.

A feeling, call it déjà-vu, makes you get out and head inside.

***

"Back already?" says the gas station attendant without looking up from his Fuentes novel.

"Pardon me?" you say, not sure why you selected such an archaic phrase instead of something simple and acceptable like "sorry" or "what."

The clerk folds the corner of the page he is reading and looks up at you with a cheery smile. He's not looking at you, but rather seeing you.

"Bottle of red, that'll be ten dollars, no tax if ya got the cash."

You put down the bottle and dive into your pocket for a crumpled ten-dollar bill. The attendant takes it and irons it out carefully.

"See ya later," he says as he deposits the bill and returns to his book.

You pause for a moment, not sure if you should question his statement before, but you decide not to. Instead, you grab the bottle and head back to your car.

It's mid-afternoon. The sun is choked by a hazy film that brings in a sick wind and drizzles from the direction of the place you do not want to go. Easing back into your car, you sit and stare at the accursed sign that sneers, leers, and mocks you: Welcome to Carver, Welcome back to Hell, Welcome back, you fucker, Welcome back, you faggot, Welcome back, you fool.

The sign is cursed because of the history beyond the border; the haunting past that you fear is still living like some nightmare creature covered in thorny black flesh that oozes and bleeds, something the sun hasn't seen since **God** and Satan walked the earth together.

A cold shiver runs through your spine and down your arms but stops at your elbows. Shaking it off, you twist the aluminum cap of the ten-dollar wine that should have been five dollars and take a series of deep drinks.

"Fuck it," you belch and tear down the two-lane road.

Daily Herald Wes

2025

Carver: 100 Years
of God

By CHRISTOPHER VIA

This weekend, the historic town of Carver, Illinois, is quietly celebrating its 100th anniversary. "It's with great pleasure that we honor our little town," says town president Susan Bloom. "Carver, much like our great nation, was founded on Judeo-Christian values. We have only God to thank!" Carver is home to one of the oldest Christian orphanages in Illinois. However, the Carver House, which once played a central role in the community, has been shuttered for nearly two decades. Rumors of...

Two

The Carver House is a house of God. That is what they say, and that is what they will always say. But the children who lived there, they would say something else. The difference in opinion between adults and children can be sifted, separated, and discovered like the various grains in a pile of sand. The mistruths are as coarse and evident as they appear. But children do not have a voice. They really never did. Not when it matters. Not when the lights go off. Not when the shadows start walking, talking, touching. Not when the moon hangs itself. Not when the piano plays something cold. The Carver House is a sonnet of secrets that only the voiceless carry. It is an orphanage of sorrow, of grotesque thoughts and practices for predators of pubescent prey.

A Thought on Orcinus Orca

One of the greatest predators to exist is the Orcinus Orca, or orca, or simply killer whale. This cetacean creature can be found on all corners of the globe. Each pod will have a variety of hunting techniques. More incredible is that they are able to teach other orcas hunting techniques depending on the location of the food source. For example, a pod of orcas hunting off the coast of Argentina will beach themselves, pretending to be helpless as they wait for the perfect moment to grab a young and/or careless seal. In Antarctica, the orca will isolate a young seal onto an iceberg and force it off said iceberg using its immensely powerful tail. The orcas, like all predators, prefer children.

***

Three

Do you remember the Bible? Try this:

Matthew 19:14

"Jesus said, 'Let the little children come to me, and do not hinder them, for the kingdom of heaven belongs to such as these.'"

I say to you that the children are being hindered. I say to you that the children have been barred from the kingdom. I say to you that the only kingdom they know is the Carver House – the house of God. Beyond the gate, through the sickly yellow peeling wallpaper, beyond the cellar, and into the attic, the rotting illusion breeds forever in secret. They love God's children and shall bathe them in his glorious teachings. That's what they say, and that's what they will always say. The predator is cunning.

CUT TO:

INT. BASEMENT BEDROOM - NIGHT

The bedroom is not a real bedroom. It's a utility closet with
cold vinyl flooring and spiders and other nameless crawling
things that hide under the shitty cot in the center of the
room.

It's nothing but a tomb for THE BOY, (6) who sits on his
hands with his head bowed as THE MAN, (50's) stands over
him with his hands on his hips.

              THE MAN
      Do you believe in God, boy?

              THE BOY
      Yes, sir.

              THE MAN
      Do you talk to God, boy? Do you
      talk to God in this house?

              THE BOY
      I do, yes sir.

              THE MAN
      That's good. That's what you say
      always, right boy?

              THE BOY
      Yes sir, I do.

The Man nods and pets The Boy's head.

              THE MAN
      Come, lay down. You're tired.

The bones of The Boy start to shake. He sinks into himself
and then out of himself.

We are him now: floating to the ceiling to join a lonely
spider in the corner.

We watch as The Man lays down next to The Boy with a sigh.

              THE MAN (CONT'D)
      What is God but dog spelt
      backwards? And what is a dog but a
      whiny carnivorous animal?

Four

You shake your head to free yourself of this memory – no, not just a mere memory, but an intrusive thought that bellows somewhere in your hippocampus, making you squirm. It came to you because you are now in front of the Carver House gate. Your windshield wipers ache from left to right, revealing glimpses of the monstrous monolith on the hill. You see it only for a moment because the rain fills the windshield before your wipers can reveal what you do not want to see again.

Five

With great hesitation, you roll down the window and reach out to the keypad speaker system.

A shaking finger selects (#) followed by the number (0).

It buzzes like a metal chair being dragged across concrete. It does this three laborious times before a click is heard, followed by breathing; that familiar heavy, hot coffee breathing that makes you wince. But then a voice on the phone rescues you from that phantom smell – Sister Hazel.

"You came," she says, her voice getting lost in the static like dust off a moth's wings.

"Yeah. Can you open the gate?"

Only the pattering of rain on the arm of your nylon jacket sleeve is heard, and the aching of the wipers. You wait another set of minutes before getting annoyed.

"HELLO?"

The breathing returns. Sister Hazel speaks, but you are certain you can hear the breathing behind her. Is it behind you?

You rub the erect hairs on your neck.

"She can't see you now. You'll need to stay in town. Come tomorrow. She can't see you. You must go. Come tomorrow, please."

A solid click, and you are left alone in front of the still-locked gate. You pull yourself back in the car, roll up the window, and curse everything, even the dust. You know you can't leave until you free your consciousness, so the best thing to do is find a hotel in town.

You reverse through the muddy trail, back onto the road, and head towards uptown Carver. The only thing on your mind is dust particles.

Dust Particles

I came across a fascinating article on the Chemical & Engineering News website. The article goes into great detail on the discovery, complexity, and hazards of dust. Apparently, dust contains thousands of compounds, including compounds we don't know of. This is because when dust leaves its resting place, it finds other additional compounds to add to itself. Essentially, it evolves into something more significant than it was before.

This gave me great pause because that means dust can carry living microorganisms. And in turn, that means dust is a living thing. In detail, dust is a house. A house that hosts these native and alien microorganisms, much like a shell hosts a hermit crab. Both the shell and the dust are one – created by God...so essentially, dust is another house of God.

***

You are on Main Street now. A series of comfortable stores, cafes, and impractical businesses pass you by as you look for a hotel. It's hard to see. Everything is covered in white noise, the kind of noise that scares you, like when your television turns on at 3:33 a.m.

Halfway down the road, you see a building with an ugly sign:

This is where you will stay. It's far and hidden from the view of the Carver House. That's at least what you think as you jump out of the car, the wine inside the pack, pack over your shoulder. You run through the rain, splash in a small lake that was created because the concrete wasn't leveled properly, and straight inside the brightly lit and contented lobby.

You walk towards the front desk, a boat of mahogany, and smile at the older lady but ignore her gray, watery eyes because behind her is a thick and heavy oil painting of the Carver House. In each of the endless windows are the small shadowed faces of what appear to be children.

"Will you be staying, drinking, or both?"

You try to look away from the painting, but your eyes are as heavy as the oils on the canvas. It's nearly impossible to pull them away.

"Uh, both please," you say dully.

"Fantastic. The room will be 55 for one night or 90 for two. The Pub is 'round the corner. Can't miss it."

"Great." You smile while pulling out the tattered leather wallet that Nayeli's brother gave you the first Christmas you spent with her: before the children, before the drinking, before the anger, and before the drama that erupts from all families like bastard thorns on a rosebush.

"If you need anything, please hit star zero, and the call will come straight to the front desk. Ask for Missy. That's me." She smiles as she hands you a keycard.

"Pub?" you say, pointing down the hallway.

"Been here before, have we?" She smiles, sits down on her 1970s office chair, and dives back into her magazine, a back issue of Time magazine from April of 2002.

The comment reminds you of the guy at the gas station, but you're tired and eager to drink, so you ignore it and squelch your way down the hallway. A few steps later, you see the frosted glass windows and cold lettering that reads quite simply: the Pub.

The doors push open quickly as you make your way inside. It's as busy as a weekday should be, so finding a seat at the bar isn't hard. You sit and glance around: chestnut shelving with a wall of liquor that shines in the dull light rack that circles the bar. Also chestnut. It's cozy.

"What will it be?" says the bartender as he shovels ice into a squared whiskey glass for a guy who sits on the other side of the horseshoe.

"Glass of cabernet"

The bartender eyes you up and down. And like all good bartenders, has you pegged faster than a therapist could. "Bottle or glass?"

"Bottle."

He leaves and returns within the minute with a bottle of cab and a glass. You give him your credit card despite not knowing the cost. He knows that it doesn't matter to you. It didn't matter for the last guy, or the one before you.

As you pour and drink, you remember the first time you had wine. It was with Nayeli at your apartment. You had four bottles that night: two reds and two whites. You both had no idea the difference. All you remember is that you wanted to drink wine after watching that movie...what movie was it? Oh yes, Sideways!

You enjoyed that movie because the main character, Miles, was a writer. You still want to be a writer, you say to yourself as you begin to thumb the aching splinter in your finger. Well, you are technically a writer, but you haven't published anything yet. Yet – that's what you used to say. It's a positive spin on 20 years of apparent waste. From childhood to adulthood. From pen to computer. You've written a dozen short stories, too many poems, and most tragically started a few unfinished novels. The splinter begins to ache as you battle with the idea of all those long and wasted years trying to figure out how to write a damn novel.

The novel is the grand achievement of any writer. It's like running a marathon. With a book under your belt, you know that you did it and can do it again. It makes you invincible to the rotting not-knowing. It's an upgrade to your armor. With it, you can slay the dragon again and again.

This is what you think. You do not know because you are not published. You are far from it. But why don't you do it? It's not because of a lack of ideas. Of course, you have ideas, but who's going to read your dumb ideas? Surely not Nayeli. And you lost the only friend you had for reasons unknown. Maybe you can go to one of those nauseating writing groups in the city where you are forced to listen to fake faces give fake advice all in the name of positivity. Why even try when you know nobody cares? Does it even matter considering you haven't completed a novel? Does it even matter considering you barely finished high school and dropped out of college? Does it even matter when you still have to sing Conjunction junction, what's your fucking function?

Did you know that the longest book ever written was by Proust? The book is called In Search of Lost Time. He wrote something like 1.2 million words. Jesus. You should really read that book. You always wanted to. You could read that until death comes a-knockin'. But what about the time between the letters, words, sentences, paragraphs, pages, and chapters? That's the time you'll find to write or maybe pay bills, argue with Nayeli, change diapers, and work. Perhaps you can write in the next life?

When did you really start writing? You think as you pour another full glass from a new bottle. Of course, it had to be after leaving Carver House.

As you think, the image of the house drips into the center of your brain and slowly cascades down over your eyes. You wipe it away and remember the story about the boxer with concrete gloves. You remember the joy you felt writing it in the fourth grade. You even made a cover with a clipart of a boxing glove. It was a fun story. A boxer wants to win a prize fight, so he puts concrete in his gloves. A sort of mystery. You think it was called "The Case of the Concrete Boxer."

You smile, drink, and pour out some more wine, but stop because you remember the teacher giving it back to you with an angry red F and a line that said, "Don't plagiarize!" You didn't know what that meant until you asked. You were confused because you only learned to read last year. You hated writing until high school.

The bottle is empty, and your head is buzzing and swirling with the weight of the idea for your novel. It's a whale. It's Ahab's white whale. It's your whale of words.

Goddamnthewordsgoddamntheartgoddamnitallandpraiseit

Your cell brings you back from your thoughts. It's Sister Hazel. Why is she calling you now? You don't like it, and you slide her red. She calls again. You repeat the steps and turn off the phone. Happy and drunk, you leave the bar and trip your way to your room upstairs.

***

The room is like all small town hotel rooms – realistic. You drop your bag and lay across the bed with a groan. Taking in a few deep breaths, you start to sleep, but your room phone shrieks you back to the light.

"God damn it," you hiss as you answer. "Wha?"

"It's me."

"How'd you ca' me?"

"It's the only place in town."

"Whatcha want," you slur.

"You are coming tomorrow to see Mommy?"

"I'm here, aren't I?"

"Yes."

Silence. Static. Breathing.

"Why didn't you open the damn gate?"

"Mommy wasn't well after she saw you."

"Saw me?"

"She was watching you from her bedroom window."

"She got sick from seeing me?"

"I dunno."

"What'd you mean dunno?" you slur, annoyed. "You fuckin' said it."

"It's late. Mommy is going to be hungry."

The phone clicks off. You toss the receiver, and it clatters against the nightstand. Your head spins dangerously. A dog barks uncontrollably down the street somewhere but it grows louder and louder until it's in your room; in your head. You eye the window and see the outline of the Carver House through the veil of night.

You vomit.

Red liquid, almost blood, hot, acidic, a never-ending vomit stream, more colors of red than you have ever seen. It pounds the carpet, splatters out, layer upon layer, it starts taking the form of some sort of abstract expressionist piece, your nose flows and adds to the puke painting, is that a house you see? It doesn't matter because a muddy wave pulls you swiftly, unceremoniously, into an ocean of shallow sleep that is deep enough to drown you.

***

You wake to the sound of birds chirping outside your window. The sun is pouring in with a sleepy day-glow yellow that paints the bedroom wall. The window is half closed, and a soft breeze spills in. The scent of fall: damp leaves washed by country rain enter your olfactory bulb, and you are whisked away to a long-forgotten memory.

You are seven and running up a hill. The hill is wet with morning dew. The sun is the same as it is in the present, gentle and warm. The very air is a Honeycrisp apple snapping in your mouth. You are on top of the hill now, wrapped in your gray scarf and wearing your dirty blue winter coat, the only coat you have, and everything is alright as you see the house below, still asleep, and you breathe in this moment, this sacred solitary moment that is yours and yours alone.

You feel the presence of something, and a balloon of panic swells inside your tummy. You sit down on the wet grass, pull your knees to your chest, and wrap your arms around them, holding on as you cry warm tears on cold cheeks as you remember the night before and all subsequent nights before when you saw Mother hug Sister Hazel with love. You crave such things so close yet so far, the distance, the size of a pine tree because that's the biggest thing you know of, and you cry harder. Suddenly you stop as the balloon inside you squirms until it bursts, and all the slimy secret things, your friends inside, slither away in all directions inside you and then they are gone, and you feel alone again.

The cold wind blows against your red cheeks, dries your lips, and hardens the wet under your nose. It brings with it a titanic feeling of loneliness that makes you acutely aware of how really, really alone you will always be. Your crystal eyes focus on the house, and you suddenly feel it and remember it and your eyes scream for help, and your mouth opens and nothing but hot air comes out, and your face is frozen as your eyes scream wide, but you still remain silent, mouth agape like some living flesh recreation of Munch's The Scream painting, the one you saw in that art book The Man has under his bed, the one that has naked girls in between the pages, the one he makes you look at with him as you both lie down on his bed, the bed that he shares with his wife, who lays between you two, holding, caressing, rubbing and back-scratching until you feel her nails scrape your epidermis so it collects under them, and you hear her sucking them like she always does while the man breathes like he can't and now your head is aching, and you snap to the present with tears on your adult face.

It takes you longer than usual to get up because of the train of thought that smashed you. The hangover is insignificant, but you start to taste your rotting mouth. The taste of your insides makes you sick, and you run into the bathroom to vomit more than the shallow puddle of wine left inside you.

Two gurgles of mouthwash, a brush, followed by a splash of cold water on the face, and you are out the door and straight into the Pub for something greasy and hot.

***

As you round the corner to the hallway with the frosted glass panels, you see that the Pub is closed. A large wooden sign hangs off the brass knobs and tells you so. Grumbling, you turn around and head back to the front desk. It's empty. You hate waiting, so you head out the front door and straight into the morning.

The hotel faces west, so everything across the street is bathed in a golden light that hugs itself against the historic structures on Main Street. It's dazzling and inspiring, even to you, as you take a right and walk through the experience making a mental note to write this scene out.

Up ahead, you see a sign that offers contribution – Carver Coffee House. It's a small establishment, and they even have a walk-up window. What a wonderful and convenient addition, you think, as you knuckle the window.

The window folds in, and a cheery-faced girl no older than 25 appears with a smile that dazzles against her black skin.

"Good morning," she says.

"Morning back," you say, trying to ignore her dangerous beauty. "I'll take a coffee and one of those egg toasters, please."

"Are you interested in our house specialty? It's called the Carver Classico."

"What makes it special – a shot of whiskey?"

"Funny!" she says, completely killing the aged joke. "It has cream and cinnamon with a dash of real vanilla. You should try it."

"Okay. I'll have it."

"That easy?"

"What's that?"

"Most people resist the upsell, but you just took it and ran with it."

"Oh, well, I don't...it sounds intriguing."

She looks at you with a new set of eyes – still big, full of expression, but this time with a hint of interest. She stares for a moment before turning around to start making the coffee. A few minutes later, she emerges with a dark red cup that steams seductively.

"That'll be 15 dollars," she says flatly.

You do a double take.

"What?"

"I'm kidding. It's on the house."

"Really? Why?" You say, genuinely surprised.

"Give me your number, and I'll tell you."

She slides her phone to you. You pause and study her face. It's radiant. Her eyes are cosmic. Your eyes fall down her smooth neck and to her breasts, which are eager and perfect from where you stand. With your right hand, you reach out and grab the coffee.

"Tempting, but I've gotta go," you smile warmly.

She stares at you, but this time, her eyes get bigger. Her sleeping eyebrows raise, and she bares her teeth like a feral animal. She begins to growl through her clenched jaws as she puts both arms to her side and begins to scream like a siren. You nearly jump out of your skin.

"What the fuck!"

The screaming doesn't stop. It somehow gets louder and more frantic. She hits the control arm of the walk-up window. It snaps shut. You're thankful for this because it muffles her banshee wails and shields you from her maddening assault as she begins to throw items, your egg toaster, for example, at the window.

You grab the coffee and begin to walk to your car while looking over your shoulder. What the hell just happened? You were polite and definitely didn't cross any lines. Jesus H, this is insane! You sip the coffee. God it's good.

You unlock your car and slide inside. Your head is echoing with her screaming. Taking a deep breath, you extract your phone from your pocket just as it starts ringing. It's Naye.

"Naye, you won't believe what just happened to me."

"Why didn't you call me last night?" she says quickly.

"I got rejected at the gate...at the house. Mother wasn't well. Got a hotel room in town. I was dead tired. But seriously, you won't believe what happened. This girl–"

"What girl?"

"I got coffee–"

"What girl?"

"Listen, I got coffee, and this girl totally freaked out on me."

"You're talking to girls while I'm sitting here watching our baby...your baby!?"

"No! It's not like that. I was just getting coffee–"

"And what do you mean you got rejected at the gate? What the hell is going on?"

The excitement of the Carver Coffee story has been executed.

"Mother didn't want to see me. She wasn't feeling well. They told me to get a room and come in tomorrow, which is today, okay?"

"You realize that you tell me nothing about your family, about your life? I have to trust you and your stories. You tell me nothing."

"Stories? You think I'm telling stories? Are you fucking kidding me!? Do you understand how much I hate this?"

"Then why go?"

You close your eyes to calm yourself and digest her pointed question. Why did you go? If you hate it so much, why did you go? You know the reason, so say it. Tell her everything. Stop living in secret.

"I...I need it to end."

"What to end?"

"Would you just get off my back? Would you please get off my goddamn back?"

Silence followed by a click.

You toss the phone on the passenger seat and rub your eyes. You're tired and finally feeling the hangover. You eye your phone before the screen shuts off. It's 8:30 AM. It's too early for all this chaos. Turning the car on, you pivot your head to check your side mirror and see the coffee girl standing down the street. She's waving at you with a happy smile.

You put the car in reverse and ignore her, because you have decided that you will be going to Carver House to get this damn trip over with.

It's been less than 24 hours and the cancer that is this town has already begun to release its poison upon you. Gripping the wheel tight, you press the gas a little too hard. You're not really sure if you're mad about the coffee girl, the call from Naye, or Carver itself. Probably all three, you think as you turn on the radio with a quick push of your knuckle.

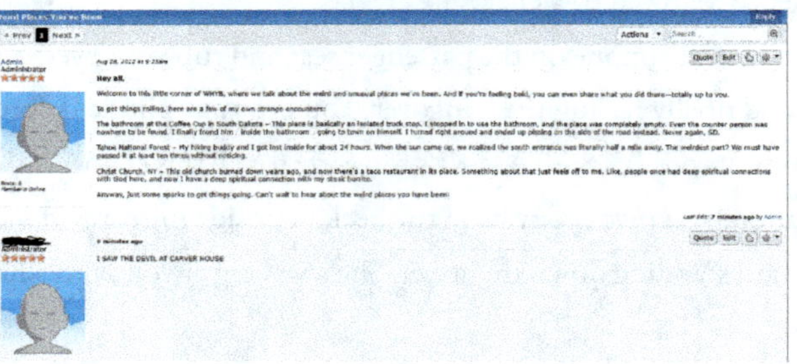

Weird Places You've Been
Reply
« Prev 1 Next »
Actions ▼ Search
Quote | Edit
Admin
Administrator
★★★★★
Posts: 8
Members Online

Aug 28, 2022 at 9:25am

Hey all,

Welcome to this little corner of WHYB, where we talk about the weird and unusual places we've been. And if you're feeling bold, you can even share what you did there—totally up to you.

To get things rolling, here are a few of my own strange encounters:

The bathroom at the Coffee Cup in South Dakota – This place is basically an isolated truck stop. I stopped in to use the bathroom, and the place was completely empty. Even the counter person was nowhere to be found. I finally found him inside the bathroom going to town on himself. I turned right around and ended up pissing on the side of the road instead. Never again, SD.

Tahoe National Forest – My hiking buddy and I got lost inside for about 24 hours. When the sun came up, we realized the south entrance was literally half a mile away. The weirdest part? We must have passed it at least ten times without noticing.

Christ Church, NY – This old church burned down years ago, and now there's a taco restaurant in its place. Something about that just feels off to me. Like, people once had deep spiritual connections with God here, and now I have a deep spiritual connection with my steak burrito.

Anyway, just some sparks to get things going. Can't wait to hear about the weird places you have been!

Last Edit: 2 minutes ago by Admin

Quote | Edit
Administrator
★★★★★

0 minutes ago

I SAW THE DEVIL AT CARVER HOUSE

Admin
Administrator
★★★★★
Posts: 8
Members Online

Quote | Edit

0 minutes ago

2 minutes ago Admin said:

I SAW THE DEVIL AT CARVER HOUSE

Uhhhhh Okaaayyyyy?

The Herald

Sunday, October 17th, 2025

Local Podcasters Die in Car

Sean Camp and Rachel Antoni, the beloved hosts of the cult podcast Fable, tragically died in a car crash late last night while en route to Carver, Illinois. The pair, known for their captivating investigations into strange and unsolved mysteries, were set to explore a series of eerie disappearances and unexplained phenomena in the small town. Their vehicle collided with a semi-truck on Route 45 just hours before they were scheduled to arrive. Both Camp and Antoni were pronounced dead at the scene. The news has sent shockwaves through their devoted fanbase, leaving many devastated by the duo's loss, whose chemistry and storytelling drew millions of listeners worldwide.

Fable, which debuted in 2020, quickly became one of the top true-crime and mystery podcasts, with Sean and Rachel's unique blend of research, suspense, and humor captivating audiences. They had recently teased a multi-part series on Carver, a town notorious for its dark past and eerie happenings. Fans have flooded social media with tributes.

Come on Up to the House

All your crying don't do no good

Come on up to the house

Come down off the cross, we can use the wood

You gotta come on up to the house

~ Tom Waits

Six

A crescendo of music rises softly until it becomes a magnificent melody of monstrous proportions. It's Toccata and Fugue in D Minor but twisted, wrong, and violent like a barbed weapon holding hanging flesh. Pounding piano, harsh strings, Gregorian chant, and music that would inspire Dario Argento to kill again, this is a cacophony of perversion and violence.

SILENCE FALLS AS...

...The gates open.

The grounds are green, the maple trees are full of flame and fire, and everything is bright under the distant but untouched October sun. The sky, not gray but blue, promises something you did not expect – hope. But hope is something you do not accept. Not here. Not inside this house, on these grounds.

The unwanted past hides beneath the faintest shadows, between the crevices of the wood shake roofs, underneath the cracks in the foundation; it is a sentient hungry spider waiting for you, knowing you would be here just the way you are now – a victim of its sticky web. Prey to its insatiable appetite.

Birds sing.

You drive through.

Ahead, in front of the house, there is a person waiting.

Seven

The sound of tires crunching the finely pebbled driveway is excellent to your ears. It's familiar and has always brought you comfort. You focus on the noise as the figure of Sister Hazel appears clearer than it ever has.

She stares at you from the top of the wraparound porch. She is wearing a heavy plaid dress. It's ugly, but it matches the house behind her. You stop the car, put it in park, and return the gaze.

The house – with its three stories, eight large rooms, five bathrooms, three towering turrets, 88 historic windows with stained glass crosses, iconic doors, black shingled roof, and dirty white and gray concrete stone siding – looks different from the last you saw it.

Memory is a liar. It holds alternate truths that constantly change, like some virus that simply wants to live. It fights to stay surfaced, so it will adapt to suit you better and make you feel safe, secure, and a little less far away from the thing that can hurt you. That is how it survives. It feeds off of the truth like a tick.

It takes you great effort to exit your car. It takes even more strength to walk up to Sister Hazel and acknowledge her presence. You would prefer her as a ghost.

"Is she better?" you say without offering emotion.

"You're here."

"You saw me driving from the house?"

"From up there, from Mommy's room." She looks up and smiles at the tallest turret with the oriel window.

Your eyes follow hers, and you gasp as you see the briefest glimpse of a white face, a fat white face, a fat, white, baggy face with beady black eyes and a large slit of a mouth. The face disappears behind the white valance drapes that move ever so slightly.

You drop your eyes, and Sister Hazel stares at you with her mouth slightly open. She's breathing dumbly as she did as a child. You think you can smell her breath: peroxide, bologna, and shit.

"Can I come in?"

Sister Hazel closes her mouth and splashes the pooled-up saliva that builds like a hot spring in her skull cavity with her tongue. She smacks her mouth open and shut, open and shut before she speaks.

"Yes, of course. It's just us, though. Nobody else came. You better come in before the rain."

You look up at the blue sky.

"I don't think it'll rain."

"It will rain," she says. "It'll storm. Mommy says it'll rain for days. You better come in before it does."

Before she can push the door open, a man, an old man, an old bent man, an old bent priest of a man, emerges. This is Father Dan. He knows you. You, after a long minute, know him again.

"Holy shit," you say with all the intentions a phrase like that could offer.

Father Dan looks at you through sunken eyes that contain a library of knowledge. He sticks out his hand and gives you a wooden rosary. The cross has an inscription: Medugorje. This will mean nothing to you until later in life.

"This is yours," he says. "You haven't found it yet but it's yours, okay?"

"Sure," you say with a smirk as you take it. "You still trying to convert the hag?"

"I'll be seeing you later."

He gives you a blessing and a prayer before pushing past you. He walks down the road, past the gate, and disappears around the bend. You can feel the cross he outlined on your forward with his thumb.

"Why was he here? You said nobody else was going to be around," you say, turning to Sister Hazel.

"I dunno."

She turns and opens the massive arched double doors that are enriched with hand-carved gilded designs. You don't think, you just follow her obnoxiously animated ponytail just like you did when you were younger; always the follower, never asking questions, just doing what you are told.

Inside, you find yourself standing once again in the cavernous foyer of the Carver House. As you cross the threshold, your eyes go dark as the transfer of light from the outside to the inside hits your pupils. You feel the pressure of them straining before they swell.

The air inside is earthy, damp, dusty and filled with particles of the past that infiltrate your nose. The blend of smells begins its journey to the black box of your body, the limbic system, by first arriving at your olfactory bulb, and then it takes a slight right to the department of amygdala for quick processing before it's sent through the hippocampus and beyond, a swirling coil that releases memories long forgotten.

Your eyes are slowly adjusting, but your vision is covered in black blemishes as you see the grand staircase. You remember running down the stairs as a child – no, being thrown down the grand staircase into darkness. You are falling, suspended in the air, involuntarily in slow motion, you feel something behind you, the atmosphere is thick, like a wet wool blanket in the summertime, whatever it is wants you and you do not want it. You see the red Persian waterfall carpet cascade below you into ebony darkness, you jam your eyes shut hoping to hit bottom, but you don't, you keep falling slowly like the burning embers of a summer campfire.

"Is it like how you remember?" asks Sister Hazel as you blink away the final splotches from your eyes and memory. You mentally note to write the experience down, but the thought and the memories cinder away like celluloid burning.

"It's dark," you say.

She smiles, "You'll get used to it."

"I doubt it."

"See, I told you it would rain."

Her eyes fall over your shoulder and through the cavity of the house.

You turn to see that it is indeed raining. How? But you don't have time to ponder this because she moves behind you, closes the doors, and locks them. Her breathing makes you step away further into the house, which forces you to study the foyer in detail.

The room is expansive, a yawning space of dark and ornate wood trim that brushes across dusty white walls that go up, up, up to a foggy glass skylight that offers no real light.

At the far end of the foyer, between two wide yet separate hallways, is the grand, three-story staircase with the cascading Persian carpet that is now frayed and stained with dark blobs of time. And at your feet, spreading out like a headache, is the marbled checkered black and white floor that is now aged, cracked, and weary with neglect.

Your eyes fall on the furniture, all original, still right there, even the red pair of damask chairs that nobody sits on.

From the corner of your vision, which is on the chairs, you see a moth fluttering by the sliding wooden door of the study you were never allowed to enter as a child. Small flakes of dust spill from the moth's fragile wings as it disappears into the dark of the room.

What is not seen is the loneliness within that seeps from the floors, the walls, and the furnishings like a cold, wet disease that can never be remedied because it has plagued every fiber of carpet and cloth, every wood cell, and every atom within this house of deprecation. You shouldn't be here.

"The house is sick," says Sister Hazel gloomily. She stands next to you, looking at the same thing she has looked at for three decades.

"Houses can't be sick."

"It started getting sick right when Mommy got sick."

This irritates you. The word mommy irritates you. Everything irritates you right now. And now the weather irritates you because a tremendous boom shakes the house. You hate thunderstorms.

"Hazel, is she up? I need to see her so I can go. I have a family."

"My niece..."

"She's fine. I need to see Mother now."

"Why can't I see her?"

"You know why, Hazel."

You catch her eyes glazing over and her eyelids becoming heavy, lost in some unknown thought, time, or space. Her lips part, and she breathes hot.

"Hazel, now, please?" you say strongly and without diplomacy.

"You can sit in the parlor. I'll go up and see Mommy. Please sit and relax. I'll only be a moment." She sings this as she speedily walks up the stairs.

You see her feet, dirty and bare, as she disappears around the landing of the second floor and up to the third. Sighing and clearing your drying throat, you walk across the marble floor to the hallway on the left of the staircase. You're fingering the beads of the rosary that you shoved in your pocket without realizing it.

The hallway archway spills out to the parlor room with oak floors that are covered in what used to be expensive rugs. An immense fireplace of brick and stone lays charred in the wall ahead of you. A huge beveled mirror encased in a brass frame hangs over the fireplace. The reflection it holds is a smear, a secret hidden behind dust and grime.

In front of the mirror, a sickly gold fainting sofa sits between a small table and a pair of lounge chairs of equal hideousness. The moth-eaten sofa is where you decide to sit.

You groan as you flump down and breathe in the dancing dust and smell on accident. Your sinuses sting, and your eyes water. With the back of your right hand, you rub your nose aggressively. Relief comes, but so does a sense of weariness. You clear your throat, flex your eyes, and look around the open parlor.

The room is dark because the bay window and the tall double-hung windows are covered by a maroon curtain. You think of getting up and pulling aside the curtain, deciding that even the storm outside would bring more light and life to the dingy dankness of the room. But the sofa is a cloud, and you are sinking, sinking deep inside because you are heavy, heavier than you remember. It doesn't stop, but you don't fight it: the sinking.

Sinking

Sinking

Sinking

Sinking

Sinking

Sinking

Your mind is transported and suspended in deep dream sleep that has complete control of you. You are now a part of the very structure of the house. Perhaps a wall, or a plank from the floor, or even...yes, that's it! You recognize it: you are inside the mirror, looking through the glass at the hazy fog of images that cannot be seen because the dust, dirt, and years of ammonia have varnished the surface like cloudy ice.

Movement stirs around you as you float in liquid mirror syrup. The outlines of things, smudges of shapes, and then a figure, a shadow of a figure, a person, enters the room and walks about.

You notice another shape, a smaller one, is next to the bigger shape. The bigger shape moves closer to you, and it becomes a large shape. Its dark aura is now misty white as it gets even closer to the mirror.

The shape extends forward; you realize it's looking at its reflection. A moment passes, and the figure pulls away. It returns to just a big shape as it moves toward the smaller shape. Another moment passes as the big shape looks down at the small shape, but the moment of stillness is brief.

The big shape grabs the small shape and hurls it across the room into something, a wide outline of darkness, maybe the couch. You hear whimpering, muffled sounds underwater. The big shape moves violently and says something in a boom of a command and the small shape whisks out of the room like a fly finding a hole in a window screen.

The big shape just stands there as your heart races from the unknown action. You don't like this big shape. You feel it in your stomach that this is a bad thing. This feeling is familiar, a warning sign forged by experience.

The warning sign flashes red hot inside you as the big shape slowly turns towards you, the mirror. It stands there. You feel your arm hairs go up, and your nipples get hard. The shape moves swiftly and with purpose toward you. It's now a large shape. It gets closer and becomes a huge fat shape, a blobulous shape that is centimeters from your surface. Another long but pan-like blob, a hand you realize, starts to rub against the dirt and grime; it rubs fast, and it rubs hard.

You can't move or scream, though you try; the only thing you can do is float and watch as the shape manically tries to clear the glass. It takes a long while, but the figure clears away a layer of filth. However, to your ease, it has only smeared the remaining gunk even more. However, your side of the world has become a bit more visible, and you see that the shape is that of a tall, fat person. This entity has cupped its foggy hands around its eyes and is now peering inside you.

The extreme close-up face is contorted, confusing, and bizarre. It instantly reminds you of that Pink Floyd face from their album

The Wall. Melted, screaming, eyeless, the mouth a massive obsidian opening with no bottom.

The fat screaming face starts to melt like the T-1000 as it presses itself against you, desperate to get inside, desperate to ooze any bit of itself on you, to become you, to own you, to terrorize you.

You scream, but no sound comes out. You try to punch, but no movement is made. Only the idea that you have done these things in your fully conscious mind remains; why are you here? Why can't you just run or fight or hide? Why, why, why, you say as the you in the mirror splinters like a spider web.

The face lunges forward and you shatter inwards, vector triangle shards of all sizes come at you slowly, but you are in a vast empty nothingness, a vacuum of space, pointless and unquantifiable, as the shards hit all of you and explode like electron missiles hitting phosphor bases. Tiny dots of the 1980s glow fill your vision and consume you totally.

You are sucked back up from the sofa and nearly fall over from the? Dream? Standing in front of you is Sister Hazel, whose doll-like face dominates your vision.

"Mommy will see you now."

Hot vomit erupts from your mouth. It's mostly bile, but the essence of the Carver Classico you drank can be detected. The sudden expulsion has you on one knee.

"Oh my God, I'm sorry. Jesus." You wipe your mouth and stand up, looking around for something to mop it up. "I need a rag or something. Jesus, I'm sorry."

"It's okay, I promise," Hazel says, looking at the sick with a cocked head. Her eyes don't blink, but they do carry an air of curiosity.

"No, please let me clean–"

"Go see Mommy. Mommy is ready to see you. I'll fix this up; I'll clean it all up. Go see Mommy before she is unwell again."

Your head starts to ache in the front; it feels like an ice cube is inside it, and you don't have the strength to argue or protest further.

"Okay. Where's the bathroom?"

Without looking away from the vomit, she points at the foyer.

"The foyer bathroom, remember?"

Turning, you leave feeling embarrassed and uncomfortable.

As you enter the foyer, you do not remember the mirror nightmare.

Inside the small foyer bathroom, you almost throw up again at the sight of the Saturday night pink wallpapered room with its floral basin and its black cross handle knobs, and everything is faded and worn and tired, which makes it even more unsettling.

Three full rotations and the black chipped faucet coughs out air, rust, and finally, clear enough water that you can splash your face and rinse your sour mouth. The cold water is nice as it finds its way around your facial crevices and nostrils. You are ready now.

Three full rotations to the right, and the water burps to a drip. You wipe your face with your shirt and decide not to look in the mirror because something tells you not to.

Exiting the bathroom, you walk over to the grand staircase and look up. The storm outside pounds the skylight above and the faint yellow lights on each floor, each landing, and each hallway barely offer a twilight of light. To your right, an eclipse of moths tango upwards, leaving winged dust snowing downward to join the other microorganisms in the air.

Breathing through your nose, your foot lands on the first step, then the second, followed by the third, and so on until you reach the first landing: 15 steps total.

The landing is six feet x six feet and features a 36" x 42" arched window with a stained glass image of a turquoise cross surrounded by 77 bright yellow shards. Outside, the gray storm makes all but the pine tree forest invisible. Looking down at the Persian rug, you feel an old burning on your knees and elbows, but ignore it and move on.

The thick wooden railing, still smooth, offers you support even though you don't need it as you climb the next 15 stairs to the second landing.

No windows here, just filthy wallpaper that has started to peel and reveal a colony of black mold. The dankness is heavy at this point. You grimace as earthy tones, heavily aged musk, and something unfamiliar but equally as horrible fills your nose. The stagnant air is a swamp despite the coolness of autumn outside and below. You quicken your pace up the final turn of stairs, this time only six steps.

You can see and smell most of the third landing where you are. The smell is a yellow puss-crusted infection on damp gauze. It's the wound ward of a hospital. It's a sweatshop, the stink under the folds of forgotten skin. You draw up your shirt over your nose so that you can breathe in your own scent.

The landing opens to a dimly lit hallway, far dimmer than the rest of the house. You try to crane your neck to see the rest without going up, but the act is pointless since you need to continue up anyway. Or do you? you think to yourself. Why not just tell Hazel what you need to tell your mother so that she can relay the message? Why not just fucking go and be done with it all?

* Because you need answers to the misery of your childhood.

Your foot lands on the first step of the final ascension and it creaks and groans. Wincing, you roll your eyes because you want to be stealthy but the house isn't going to let you. The second step groans and creaks louder, and so does the third, the fourth, and the fifth, but not the sixth which is the landing. Your heart is racing, not from the climb, but from the reality that just hit you.

This is it. This is what you came for. To see your dying mother and snip away the remaining umbilical cord, navel string, funiculus umbilicalis, flesh rope, the tether of life, the Wharton jelly highway so that you may live once again as a man on his own without the jerk of the past reminding you of everything you need not remember.

The putrid smell farts away all the introspective thoughts that you just had. It's impossible to focus or be mentally competent. You hope to get used to this fetid atmosphere, but your leg autonomously drops back onto the fifth stair in an attempt to get the rest of you down and away.

"Is that you?" says a heavy voice laced with the frills of a young girl. The voice crawls down the hallway from a door you cannot see.

A wave of fear, the fear that you felt as a child, hits you unadulterated, with no filter, screaming, a shrieking guitar noise that lifts you up and slowly drags you forward, down the hallway, to the oak wooden door at the end of the hallway.

Is the door opening, or was it already open? The fear has scraped your short-term memory, so you aren't sure.

Heavy breathing escapes like noxious gas from the black sliver between the frame and the slab. Your nervous system has become hyperactive, and you start to tremble and shake. A moth, maybe one from the rising eclipse you witnessed before, pushes past you and slips inside the room that you will be entering momentarily.

In a nauseous daze, you push open the door and enter the room. This is what you see, and this is what happens:

- The room is the master bedroom.

    ○ It's dark and gloomy. All eight of the windows are

shrouded with dark drapes.

- ○ Stacks of chaos are everywhere. Including inside the six-foot fireplace.

- In the center of the 14-foot vaulted-ceilinged room, against the north wall, is a massive four-poster bed draped in thin floor-length white canopy curtains.

  - ○ In the center of the bed, sitting up, is a sweating planet-sized blob of a woman dressed in a yellowing nightgown.

    - Her hair is tufts of thin curls that are scattered across her tightly wrapped skin like a poorly maintained crop.

    - She smells of the house.

- You glitch. You literally glitch at the sight of her.

CUT TO:

(Take two) In a nauseous daze, you push open the door and enter the room. This is what you see, and this is what happens:

- The room is the master bedroom.

  - ○ It's dark and gloomy. All eight of the windows are shrouded with dark drapes.

  - ○ Stacks of chaos are everywhere. Including inside the six-foot fireplace.

- In the center of the 14-foot vaulted-ceilinged room, against the north wall, is a massive four-poster bed draped in thin floor-length white canopy curtains.

- In the center of the bed, sitting up, is a sweating planet-sized blob of a woman dressed in a yellowing nightgown.

  - Her hair is tufts of thin curls that are scattered across her tightly wrapped skin like a poorly maintained crop.

  - She smells of the house.

  - She smiles with her cola-caked yellow teeth and her eyes reflect like phantasmal orbs of light.

- You glitch again at the sight of her.

CUT TO:

(Take three) In a nauseous daze, you push open the door and enter the room. This is what you see, and this is what happens:

- The room is the master bedroom.

  - It's dark and gloomy. All eight of the windows are shrouded with dark drapes.

  - Stacks of chaos are everywhere. Including inside the six-foot fireplace.

- In the center of the 14-foot vaulted-ceilinged room, against the north wall, is a massive four-poster bed draped in thin floor-length white canopy curtains.

  - In the center of the bed, sitting up, is a sweating planet-sized blob of a woman dressed in a yellowing nightgown.

- Her hair is tufts of thin curls that are scattered across her tightly wrapped skin like a poorly maintained crop.

- Her smell is the house.

- She smiles with her cola-caked yellow teeth and her eyes reflect like phantasmal orbs of light.

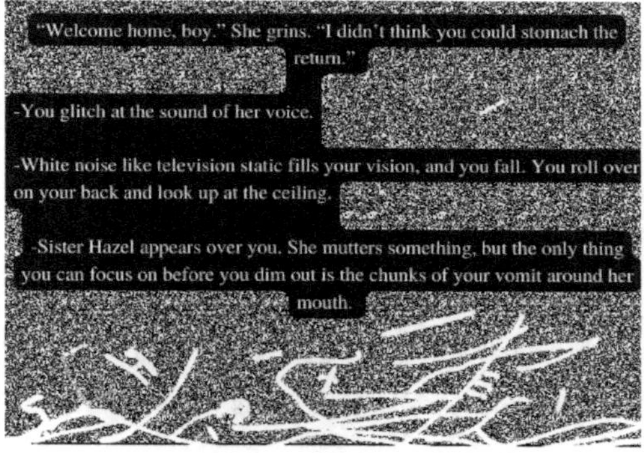

Eight

A Widening Thought Written on Labor Day Weekend at 4:30 AM

What does it mean if you wake up in the past? Is it a malfunction of the brain? Like a match being struck underwater and, in some impossible way, sparks for a flash of a second. Or does it mean that the other side, the dream side, is a place so vast and unknown that the mere idea of it makes anything possible? A fantasy world of rainbow slides that take you to sun-yellow happy places of green hills and blue skies with fruit-colored birds that swim in the scents of summer, or it could be the doomed elevator that goes down, down, down to the places you do not want to go, places that hurt and burn and gnash and crash and yell and apply pressure in all the wrong places. The doors, the windows to the other side are endless, and only the ones who travel there can understand this, but nobody who survives it can remember it, because even the golden lining of clouds and the promise of the crepuscular rays of something good this way comes is too dynamic for the mind to handle. It's an equation the world has tried to solve.

From the natives that practice the art of peyote to the LSD-dripped rocker, the answer has always been sought but never found, only a taste, a skimming, like a gliding bird of water that can seemingly fly but, in truth, cannot fly at all, not really, not ever. So, the manual to this dilemma has never been written completely; instead, words have been stitched together from poems, prose, and essays. Some provide pages while others provide only single words, and other contributions have been added by the stroke of a brush, painted visions that cover canvas or corners of canvas. Nonetheless, it is all part of this living journal that hopes to be completed into a comprehensive guidebook, an SOP of sorts for those who find themselves inside the equation. Sixty-four thousand years have passed since the first contribution to said equation. And now, we, the people, understand this mathematical machination for what it is. It's an impossible equation because you have no idea what side of sleep you are on. Right now, are you really reading this? If so, which YOU is reading this? The YOU from when you are dreaming, or the YOU from five minutes ago? Where did that person go? The one who started reading this? Prove to me that the YOU who read the posing question above is the same person who is reading this now. You can't. You can only think back to reading any of this, but you can't point that person out to me. It's impossible because that person does not exist. They can't exist because you only exist in reality, and reality is only real in the present, in the now. The past is nothing but a series of counterfeit imaginations of what happened in the present. It lies to help you. It protects you – both the bad and the good of your reality. But I ask again, what does it mean if you wake up in the past?

A Widening Question...

A	B	C	D	E	F	G	H	I	J	K	L	M
				16								

N	O	P	Q	R	S	T	U	V	W	X	Y	Z

    "___   ___ ___ ___ ___   ___ ___
      9   13 16 6 22   22 20

    ___ ___ ___ ___ ___   ___ ___   ___ ___ ___
     3   21 16 16 1   9   6   22 17 16

    ___ ___ ___ ___ ___ ___ ___   ___ ___ ___
     1   15 16 3 16 6 22   8   6 23

    ___ ___ ___ ___   ___ ___   ___ ___
    13 20 19 16   7   1   9   6

    ___ ___ ___   ___ ___ ___ ___
    22 17 16   1   8   3 22

    ___ ___ ___ ___ ___   ___ ___ ___
    13 17 16 15 16   13   8   3

    ___ ? "
     9

You wake up in the past. You're six years old. You are playing with a toy truck that Father Dan gave you a few days ago when he visited your sick Great Babushka, who is still sick but active and cooking borscht in the kitchen downstairs. The smell is not describable because borscht, the holy winter soup, is its own smell, plays with your nose, and pulls you from your oval woven rug.

With a happy smile, the kind that curls the corners of the lips like a cartoon character, you softly creak down the stairs, tip-toe across the hall, and shuffle into the kitchen. Your mouth waters, and you swallow with delightful hunger.

Babushka is chopping away at things and stirring, chopping away and stirring; it's kitchen music, and you like it. It inspires you to speak.

"Privet, Babushka!"

She straightens up and slowly turns to you. Her blue eyes with red bags blink at you; they blink away with what is probably dementia or just hate, and she roars at you in her native tongue. It translates to something like, "You are not Valter's son! You shit, a little boy gets out!"

You turn to flee, but a knife is thrown just as you start taking off. The knife point stabs you in the lower right side; it inserts in you like a hot knife in butter but very hot, too hot. The irony is beyond you, but the knife thrown was a butter knife indeed.

She goes back to the holy borscht as you scream, cry, and bleed.

You search for your mother throughout the entire house, the big house, the Carver House, The House, The House, the house you grow to hate with each empty room discovered, each sour-smelling hallway explored, yet still you can't find her, for she's busy with Father Dan somewhere deep inside, hidden, and so you run back upstairs to your room, only to realize, with a pang of regret, that you dropped your truck – the only toy you have – and you cry, bleed some more, and fall asleep on the oval woven rug, like a cat, or a dog, or some animal forgotten, unloved, untouched and unwanted.

***

You wake up, and your shirt is stuck to your back; the blood has dried and is holding your shirt hostage. You look out the window and see that it's dark outside. Voices, laughing, call you down. Rubbing the dry snot from your nose, you solemnly go downstairs.

Mother, Father Dan, the red-haired man who calls himself Cousin Richie, Sister Hazel, and Great Babushka are drinking and eating borscht. You take a seat between Cousin Richie and Sister Hazel. You feel your mother looking at you with ugly eyes.

"Your shirt, what happened?"

"Babushka threw a knife at me."

Eyes ping-pong between you and Babushka as Mother sucks her cigarette, menthol, between her sausage fingers.

"Babushka?"

Babushka waves her hands in the air and speaks in broken English, confirming this and advising that you do not look like her son, and that means you are not her grandson, and that means you are a stranger, and strangers should not be sneaking inside the kitchen to watch Babushkas make borscht.

Your mother nods and tells you to eat. You take the paddle of a spoon, dip it in the small bowl, and eagerly slurp down, only for your mouth to experience nothing but the cold, wet soup that should be hot because, again, it's winter's holy soup. You whimper and eat anyway.

A few clinks and dips of rye bread, and you're finished. Cousin Richie stares at you. You grow colder than the soup as he tells you he brought his red convertible, and he wants you to take a ride with him. He's going to help you with that ouchie on your back.

He grabs you by your hand and takes you to a room, not yours, as your mother laughs at something Father Dan says who eyes you with great sadness, the kind of sadness you see in Christ on the cross in some churches.

Carver House
Carver, Illinois
August 1994

Dear Me,

Please, if you find this, read it before they come downstairs! You need to listen to me. What's about to happen is not your fault. Please believe that. You don't have to do what I did. The blame isn't yours alone.

They will hurt you. The dream you have—the one where you feel like you're being eaten from the toes up—it's not a dream. He likes to lick them, suck on them. And he tries—oh God, he tries to eat us.

You have options. You can fight back. You can run and never look back. Whatever you do, don't believe her lies—she's a master of them. She hates everything about you. No matter how sweet she sounds, don't trust her.

Don't go into her room. Don't let HIM into yours.

If you're reading this, you need to RUN. Now!!

Sincerely

Nine

***

A colossal boom shakes the house, and you wake up in a bed, in the house, in the present. You're drenched in sweat and confused. Your hands fumble around for your cell phone, but they can't find anything; panic sets in, but only briefly because the phone is in your pants pocket, not on your nightstand at home because you aren't at home; you are at your mother's house, remember?

Your tongue feels like sandpaper. It takes you another round of thunder to remember what happened. You saw Mother and passed out, but why?

Swinging your legs over the rickety bed, you stand up and quickly sit back down because a whirlpool of dizziness hits you. Low blood sugar?

The door opens as you steady yourself. It's Sister Hazel, who looks worried and scared, like a little girl who's meeting a friend for the first time.

"I'm sorry. Are you okay?"

"What happened?" you say, massaging your temples.

"I'm not sure. I was downstairs, and I heard a big thump, so I came up. You passed out. Mommy was worried sick, so she had me put you in one of the spare rooms."

"Aren't all the rooms spare?" you say dryly.

"Cousin Richie left, and all the other kids left too, so I guess so."

"That happened a long time ago, Hazel. You speak as if it happened yesterday."

"I miss them."

You put up your hand to stop her from talking further. "I feel like shit. I don't have the energy to talk about all that, okay?"

She nods.

"My blood sugar probably dropped or something. I need to eat."

"Mommy made food. She's waiting for you in the dining room. It's going to be delicious!" says Hazel with a smile.

"She made food? How long was I out?"

"Just for a while," she says as she leaves.

"Right, whatever." You stand up and follow her out of the room down a long hallway littered with photos that don't include you. The parade of pictures leads to the dining room. Sister Hazel and you enter.

A roaring fire lights the room in a warm and welcoming light. The cherry wood table, long enough for ten people, glows. Sitting at the head of the table, in what appears to be a custom-made chair, is your mother. Her face is dolled up. She looks like Baby Jane.

"Well, good evening, sleepyhead."

You sit down and try not to stare at how gigantic she is.

"Hi, sorry about the drama, I guess my blood sugar dropped."

"Don't apologize. And nothing beats the downies better than your favorite – borscht!"

Sister Hazel places a large bowl of steaming soup in front of you. You stare at its chunky redness. The smell opens your saliva glands, and your mouth floods.

"I had a dream about borscht," you say as you dive in.

Mother watches you with her blue-shaded eyes.

"I haven't had this in twenty years, Mom. Thank you."

"Thank you," she says with a soft smile. "I'm sorry I waited this long. I really am. Please, let us eat without remorse."

Sister Hazel sits in the center seat of the table. She folds her hands to pray and looks around. You and Mother follow suit.

"Heavenly Father, bless this meal that sits before us, bless this home that houses us, and bless us with all the things dwelling in it, amen."

Amens are muttered, and everybody eats. The clinking and slurping of borscht dance with the crackle and roar of the fireplace, and suddenly, you get a heavy feeling of comfort. A comfort you never felt before, because it wasn't there as a child. The hairs on your arms rise as you look around.

There she is, your mother, who after all these long years, finally made you a goddamn bowl of hot soup and offered the most sincere declaration ever with a single sorry. Her words came when the chemicals in your brain and body were a bit off, so they landed softly on your shoulder and cooed sweeter than you could have expected.

Words are white blood cells, they can heal all wounds; words are treaties that can end wars; words are the bricks of a church that can save souls; words are seeds that, if planted, can grow and sustain life. Sweet words that roll off the tongue and pass through the lips of a mother can make a man or woman feel like a child sitting at a table, laughing, sharing, sharing food, sharing love, sharing everything that the soul needs. It's the way it should always be; it's the way it never was growing up, growing old, growing cold. But that was then, and this is now; this is reality – the holy borscht, the child in manhood, the sister of happiness, the mother of penance.

This feeling that encompasses you is intoxicating. It makes you feel a type of horny. A non-sexual horny, the kind that makes you feel giddy, stupid, happy, and eager to chat with strangers; the kind that makes you look your mother in the eye with empathy between slurps of delicious soup.

"I'm glad I came."

"Are you?" she says as a bit of soup runs from the corner of her mouth. "Perhaps you're still a little dizzy."

"No, really, I am. This opportunity..."

The words fail you for an instant because the moment that was impossible before is happening now. The moment you dreaded at home, in the kitchen, is laid out in all its glory.

"...I guess we both have a thousand questions, huh?" you finish with an affirming nod.

"Hmmm," Mother purrs as she rips a chunk of rye bread and baptizes it before shoving it in her mouth. "Where to start, hmmm? Hazel, do you have any ideas?"

Sister Hazel smiles from the side of her mouth, embarrassed but pleased that she was called first because she already has questions bubbling in the front of her mind.

"Thank you, Mommy!" She turns to you, "Do you still pray to Jesus and God and the saints?"

The question is unexpected but heavy. You'd figure the first round would be about hobbies, maybe career situations or aspirations, not about religion.

"Uh, well, I haven't in some time. But it's always in the back of my mind."

"Oh, well, you don't have to worry about God in the back of your mind anymore. He's always here with us, always. Isn't that right, Mommy? He's under our feet."

"Under our feet?" you say.

"He's everywhere," Mother chimes in. "What Hazel is saying is that you can see him when you want to during your stay here."

"Right, well, I don't think I'll be staying long. I'm probably leaving tomorrow morning. Gotta get back to the family, you know."

"Oh, I don't think so," laughs Mother as she picks up her bowl, tiny in her hands, and swallows whatever wasn't spoonable. "We're looking at flash floods and severe storms all night, Sweetness."

Your gut tightens at this, but you don't want to seem rude. The good feeling, the invisible hug sort of feeling, is still strong, and you do not want to lose it. "I guess it's best I stay here unless things turn over."

"I believe that's a good idea," says Sister Hazel eagerly.

You take in more soup as you lob a question. "I saw Father Dan when I got here. What's he up to nowadays?"

"Paying his respects to the house," says Sister Hazel, looking down at her bowl.

"You mean paying respects to you and Mother?"

Sister Hazel chews the skin on her lower lip. You watch as she catches a small peeled flake between her front tooth and her incisor. She bites and tugs it until it tears, and a small bead of blood forms.

"So, boy," burps Mother as she pushes away her plate, "how's my granddaughter?"

This is a sensitive subject for you. The day you found out you were having a baby, a heavy shift occurred inside the deepest levels of your being. You decided to build a fortress inside of you so that the past could not infiltrate and haunt you anymore.

From each stage of the pregnancy to after the birth, the past would assault your fortress, attempt to ruin you from the inside, tear you down, brick by brick, and smash every atom from every stone. But you held fast, and you held strong. You resisted; you fought back because of the promise that you made. A promise for her, your daughter, to live amongst the light and learn about the darkness rather than live in darkness and learn about the light, as you did. You wanted her to paint her own masterpiece, compose her own songs of life, and write her own successes and failures without human corruption lurking behind her sleeping eyes, in front of her waking eyes, all of it. But here is the question offered to you, a question that is either a cannonball of destruction or a tool that will end the great fortification of fatherhood.

"She's fine," you finally say.

"Why don't I get to see her?"

Be strong, be the diplomat that you are.

"I understand you, Mother. But I'm not ready for that. You and I still have a lot to chat about, you know?"

"I guess we do, don't we? It's hard to look back and talk about what you saw...what happened, isn't it?"

"Yes, but I'm here now, with you and Sister Hazel, to talk about everything so that we can understand each other and maybe bring peace between us all."

Mother makes a face as if stomach acid hit her heart. She pounds on her chest plate. The force of the blows jiggle her breasts and shake the table. She belches something fierce.

"Let it all out, boy."

"Do you know what Cousin Richie did to me?"

Expelling this weight makes you feel seven pounds lighter. You sigh and breathe in the fading steam of borscht.

"Cousin Richie...Cousin Richie?" says Mother with deep thought. A light bulb goes off in her head, and she snaps her fingers. "Ah, of course, Cousin Richie with the red convertible, what a sweet thing he was to you."

"Mother, he hurt me," you say boldly.

Mother stares at you. Her eyes reflect the dancing flames from the fireplace, but she sees you and hears you. "And what else, boy?"

"Why did you let Babushka hurt me?"

"She didn't like you. What was I supposed to do?"

"Why? Why didn't she like me?"

"You don't know, boy?" says Mother, looking at you with a wry smile. "Truly?"

You shake your head, no.

"What do you remember about your past?" questions Mother with big, pouty lips.

"I don't know...I mean, my past is like a slowly burning photograph. It's charred, fragmented images of something not fully seen. When I look back, I feel sadness. I feel lonely as I try to put the image together in my mind. I wanted you, Mother. I wanted my family to love me. And after the yearning comes the fear. It bubbles up from somewhere deep inside, you know? Old, gaseous boiling bubbles that burst, releasing pain and hurt from all that you did to me, that the family did to me. Mother, do you know what happened to me? What they all did to me?"

"I remember you lied about it. I remember you got Cousin Richie in trouble. So much trouble, boy, that he hanged himself...that sweet man hanged himself...killed himself because of you."

"No, Mother, it wasn't a lie. This house killed me when I was a child. You killed me when I was a child, but I am here now, as a man, looking for resurrection."

Mother licks the corner of her mouth and expels something from her nose. Sister Hazel rocks in her chair.

"Is that all, boy? What else do you have to get off your chest, hmmm?"

A sweater of uncomfortable anger covers you, but you focus on her question. It's her way of saying she is listening and letting you have the floor. It must be her way of making peace. So peace comes only after war, and war contains multitudes.

"What happened to my dad?"

Without missing a beat, Mother replies.

"He died."

"I know, but when?"

"Last month."

"Why didn't you say something to me? I needed to talk to him," you cry out in disbelief.

"Because I want you to suffer, even now."

"What....why?" you say as you sink into your chair. Your shoulders fall. Your back hunches as the weight of her dominance weighs upon you. You feel like that kid again.

"Because, boy, you have ruined this house of God with your so-called innocence. Do you understand?"

She stares at you, and you stare at her. She has the high ground; you can feel it. Right now, you are empty in thought because she blew up anything inside.

She continues.

"I think I should tell you something, though I wanted to hold on to it, savor it for longer, it is the sweetest bit of something that I have. Alas, it's time for me to give it up, to share with you. I think you deserve it, alright?"

"Alright?" you say without hiding your total perplexity.

"Good. This house of God was an orphanage, boy, as you know. That's why you had so many cousins and other little shits around when you were younger, for a time, until they all left, understand? Father Dan was the teacher and the priest here, do you remember? Good. All the kids left because they ran away, went to other foster homes, or got adopted; it's the cycle of an orphanage, understand? Good. Well, time passed by, and the only creature remaining was you, do you understand? You aren't my boy; you are just a boy. You aren't my son, heavens no; you're a leftover chunk that fell from your drug-loving mother's gaping fuckhole, a squirting gift from your recently deceased murderer of a father, do you understand? You are an orphan. Sister Hazel is the only child I bore, and one of the other foster kids blessed me with her, understand?"

The sting from her vivacious, vicious, vomiting, vexing words fills the room like shit fills a diaper. The only thing you can do is shake your head and hold back the welling tears building under your lids.

"It doesn't matter if you forgive me, boy. You ruined this house; you ruined my family. But what I want to know, and be honest with your mommy (she giggles at this), what on God's green earth made you come back here, to this house of horrors as you dubbed, to see me, Satan's fat whore, as you called me some time ago?"

Not even the fire made a sound. Everything is dead silent as you sit looking between Mother and Sister Hazel, who avoids your eyes.

"I, uh, what, uh...do you...I'm confused?" the words stumble out of you like they did when you were a kid. A train that derails and wrecks at each word, each scared uh and um.

The table shutters as Mother rests her giant elbows between her bowl and plate. She creates a flesh pyramid with her hands and rests her saddlebag of a chin under her chewed-up fingernails.

She leans closer to the table. The firelight dances across her face like Halloween. The silence feels like thunder. The atmosphere starts to change; it becomes hot and heavy. That feeling of giddiness and boyish joy is sucked – no, ripped out of you like a fish is ripped out of the sea. You are exposed, set up, and caught like a moth in a corner spider web. All you can do is gaze into the fire-lit face of your mother.

She screams:

"WHAT The FUCK are YOU doing in MY Fucking

HOUSE!!!!!!!!!!!!!!!!!!!!!!!!!!!!"

Your spoon clatters inside the bowl as you literally get pushed back by her assaulting voice.

Mother begins to beat the table with her ham-sized fists like some sort of engorged dictator. Spit flies from her mouth as she bellows like a foghorn; it's a deep bellow, a scratchy bellow, a man or a beast's bellow, and she starts weeping.

Sister Hazel shoots up and starts weeping as well. She grabs you with a vice-like grip on your bicep and drags you away down the hall into the bedroom in which you woke.

"What the fuck is going on!? What the fuck, Hazel!"

"I'm sorry. I'm so sorry. I wanted to see you again. Please don't be mad!"

"Don't be mad. Jesus, did you see that...that thing in there? She's insane! You're insane...fuck this, I'm out of here!"

You search for your keys but can't find them. You turn to Hazel, but the pair of you freeze as tremendous booms sound from the house. These booms are not from the convenient thunderstorm outside but from inside the house, something clearly human as they come in waddling steps.

BOOM! BOOM!

"Hazel, where are my keys?!" you yell.

BOOM! BOOM!

"Hazel, where are my fucking keys!"

BOOM! BOOM!

Sister Hazel's eyes glaze over, and her mouth opens as she slowly starts to walk backward into the darkening hallway. You can't see her mouth move, but you clearly hear her say, "Mommy is coming."

"Hazel, fuck, HAZEL!" You try to grab her, but she's gone, and you are alone in the small room staring at the flickering hallway of darkness.

BOOM! BOOM!

The lights shutter off, and you start to weep in fear.

BOOM! BOOM!

With a frigid hand, you reach for the doorknob, but the door is ripped open completely by the ham-like hands of your mother, whose enormous frame fills your vision.

Two massive arms grab you and pull you into the darkness, into her sweating chest, into the stink of her. You can't breathe, and you are weak as she hugs you and drags you for what feels like forever, down and to the right and down again, into the cold basement room of your childhood.

You are thrown onto the bed of darkness, and the door slams shut, and the sound of a hundred locks is heard, and your heart races in your neck, and you can't breathe, and you are getting dizzy again, and you are in cosmic blackness, darkness so unnatural that you can feel it slither around your body like a snake that wraps around you and chokes you as it pushes down your esophagus into the pit of your stomach and beyond, and not even your subconscious can speak as you pass out from fear, but not before the darkness illuminates the naked orange-haired man who is smiling in the corner of the room.

THOUGHTS ON HOUSES LIKE THE CARVER HOUSE

All houses have secrets; little children are blind and deaf to them. They are nothing but television static or low murmuring chatter outside your window. This is the way of things so that the scabby kneed ones, the messiah loved ones, and the innocent ones can continue to live. But some houses, like the Carver House, like to gossip to the children and share little half-truths and reveal glimpses of things that they hide. It's not widely understood why these houses, some say living, do this. Perhaps it is for mere entertainment, or perhaps the house has held on to too many secrets in its memories that they seep out of the walls, out of the floorboards, out of the very foundation in which the deepest darkest secrets go, down to the galaxy of insects below, that crawl to the surface, creeping towards the pattering of little feet above, the feet of those who are able to hear the houses bemoan scandalous stories, little treats that will splinter the mind of children so that they stop and stare and ponder and try to make sense of the sticky world, the grinding world, their world, their little world that shouldn't understand such things and will not when the house speaks to them. But all words are fresh synapses that will fester just as the house – not all houses, but houses like the Carver House – want to. It is true that the Carver House takes great pleasure in the madness it holds and hides. It is true that the Carver House grows great black rot so that the secrets can spread faster. It is true that the Carver House was once a house of God, the Christian God, but now another God, and underneath it lies a secret so ancient that it started to push past the foundation and the dirt so that it may live immortal, like a word that exists even when we do not know it. This secret beneath the feet started to form into a magnificent structure. That is what all secrets are: magnificent structures with many rooms and many purposes, and each of these rooms expands into hallways that grow even deeper so that even more rooms can hold even more secrets. Oh, so many secrets to worship that this structure below takes a familiar shape because it has a familiar purpose that all mankind understands – to worship the secret, in the secret structure below, the secret cathedral.

Eleven

Time passes slowly when darkness surrounds it. It is as if the absence of light strangles the very idea of time itself. The strangulation of time kills all things that follow the construct, but most of all, it affects man. For what is life without keeping time? It is nothing, a blank canvas with no point, rhyme, or reason.

It would be pointless to live this way, you think, as you close your eyes for no reason at all. You consider suicide or at least you allow the thought to cross your mind, but you know, deep inside, that you can't because an image flashes in your head like a strobe light.

The image flashes faster and faster until it becomes constant and glows. The glowing image of a heart with a sword through it burns inside your mind. You have no idea what this image is or how it surfaced, but you understand something now; perhaps your situation, to accept your situation, to survive your situation, to confront your situation as an adult in the basement darkness.

You open your eyes and stand up, searching through the abyss of the room that knew you as a child, but not as an adult; not as you are now. This is the advantage that you carry with you like a torch as your memory of childhood fear is replaced by the confidence of manhood.

"Cousin Richie," you say aloud.

The darkness does not speak.

"Cousin Richie!" you say louder.

The darkness does not speak.

"Cousin Richie!" you bellow, "So help me God, reveal yourself!"

The darkness does not speak but it moves like a wave, as if something crawls underneath the blanket of blackness. The wave reaches you and from the darkness, two long pale arms covered in freckles grab you and crawl all over your body, your face, trying to remove your clothes. A hiss of a voice slithers out.

"God? What is God but dog spelled backward? And what is a dog but a whiny carnivorous animal?"

You fight the arms off as if they were flames. And they burn you like flames. You scream and fall and roll and push away until you escape the arms that live in the darkness.

The image of the heart, the pierced heart, glows immaculately inside you.

Standing up again, you ball your fists in anger. Your knuckles feel like they're going to break from the pressure, and your heart is a drum roll as you call out again, but this time with a lion's roar.

"Richie!"

The wave returns, this time to your right. But instead of just arms, the naked orange-haired man, in his sweaty completeness, steps out from a slit of darkness. Out steps Cousin Richie with open arms and a smile that cracks the skin; out steps Cousin Richie the tickler; out steps Coustin Richie the flake eater; out steps Cousin Richie the bastard.

You take a step back as his smile expands. It expands to the point of impossibility. His jaw grinds open as it reaches the ground. His mouth is now a garage that can fit a small child inside it with ease. Pools of spit spill out of his mouth as his tongue lazily flips around like a fish out of water. A slobbering wet noise hisses out.

"I'm going to eat youuuuuuuu. I'm going to eat youuuuuu, and then I'm going to eat your little candy drop daughterrrrrrrrrrrrr."

You can't fight this. How can you fight such a ridiculous thing, such a monstrosity? You simply can't fight ghosts.

But then you realize something as your heart threatens to burst from your chest. You remember something about memories: Cousin Richie hanged himself in this room nearly twenty years ago, and ghosts only attach themselves to memories because you birthed them and laid them on the memory like an egg sack, waiting to be born. Then you remember Neville from Harry Potter, General George Patton, the glorious image of the heart that still shines inside, and the stoic Nayeli and the gift of life that she gave you.

With this understanding, you walk towards the phantasmagoria in front of you, towards the slobbering oral cavity cave, and enter the mouth willingly.

The mouth closes around you. The humidity inside reminds you of the time you and Nayeli went to Quintana Roo, Mexico. It was the first time you experienced a tropical climate. You loved that sort of climate. The way it soaked to your bones and kept you warm, the way it found itself deep inside your DNA, touching your ancestral past. You grow sleepy inside this humid mouth, so you lay down on the soft tongue and sleep without dreaming.

(Note: Start begging for prayers.)

Twelve

You are awakened by a knock on the basement door; the sound of endless sliding and turning of locks brings you a relief that you did not know existed.

The darkness is cut severely by the weak light from the hallway. You do not know what time it is, but you feel that it has been days since you were shut into this room. You squint and see Sister Hazel emerging from the doorway.

"Mommy is sleeping."

"How long have I been here?" you say, standing up, feeling the stubble on your face.

"Just the night. Mommy got mad at you. She gets like that. I'm sorry," whimpers Hazel.

"She was always like that, Hazel."

"She's sick. She isn't well."

"You told me that she wanted to see me. You told me that she's dying. You lied to me!"

Sister Hazel shrinks and hangs her head. She can feel your rage.

You want to keep yelling at her. Let her know that she is worthless to you, that this was all a mistake, and that she and her mother can rot in hell forever because that's where they belong. You don't. Instead, you sigh at the pathetic sight of her cowardice, of her lifelong childish ways, and think of your daughter and her smile and her hugs and kisses.

"I need to get out of here, Hazel."

"You can't," she says.

"Why?"

"Come with me, and I'll tell you everything."

She raises her small hand to you. You look at it and take it. You haven't felt her cold, porcelain flesh since you were kids. It's not a hand that you care to hold, but you need to so you can get out of this room.

You are pulled through the basement, up a set of cold concrete steps, down a dim hallway you don't remember, and up another set of stairs that take you to Sister Hazel's room.

Inside, everything is a soft bubblegum pink and still very much the same as you remember it. Even the pink dollhouse in the corner by the window remains the same. This sickens you.

You walk over to the window and look out. The view is crippling as you remember that mother's window is directly across from Hazel's. No hint of grass, trees, or nature, just the cold glass window of Mother's room.

"Why did you bring me here, to the house?" you say, turning your attention to the dollhouse.

The bed pffttts as Sister Hazel sits on it.

"You've seen things in the house, haven't you?" she says factually.

"I see a lot of things," you say sharply, "why did you bring me here?"

"The house is sick," she replies. "The house is sick, and it told me that it wanted to have you again."

The way she says this, or perhaps just the fact that she said it, makes your stomach squirm. You want to slap her and tell her to shut up about the house and that she's crazy, but you don't because the rock that has dropped inside your stomach tells you that, somehow, this is true.

You say nothing as you crouch down and look inside one of the windows of the dollhouse. Inside, small-scale figurines kneel and pray in front of an even smaller house. The figures are of a woman, a girl, and a boy.

"Is what she said true, Hazel?"

"I love you."

You turn around and see Sister Hazel standing naked, her legs spread, revealing both vagina and penis. Arms out, her thin boy-like breasts sag, and her nipples are erect like spires from a church.

"I don't love you," you say, looking her deep in the eyes and not at the sin of a body you know too well.

"Let me love you again, please?" she whimpers, looking at your waist, at your manhood behind the cloth.

"Love me? You hurt me, a child; you stained me, ruined me with your filth. I hated you the day I saw you. I hated you then, and I hate you now."

The feeling, the same feeling you received inside the basement room, the feeling that shielded you inside the ghost below, returns tenfold.

Hazel's eyes gloss over, this time white as eggs, and she breathes heavy, rotting breath. She speaks, but in a voice that fluctuates from man to woman to girl, like someone skipping through an old radio. "You can't really hate, not really, not truly, not like how Mommy hates you. You are already mine, I've had you. You'll always carry me around like an ache, I'll never go away, and you'll never go away because I still have you. I'll always have you."

Hazel starts to drip from between her legs. The mucus-like liquid leaks down her thin thighs, and a long, sinewy strand of the clear stuff hangs from both of her sexual organs.

Slowly, she turns and walks out of the room. Something tells you to follow, and you do.

You follow her down the hallway that you came from. But instead of taking a right to the grand staircase, you take a left and face a small wooden door. It appears to be a small closet, a broom or linen closet.

Hazel grabs the small brass knob and opens it to reveal that it is indeed a linen closet, occupied by countless engorged moths. Eager to escape, they flutter away as you watch Sister Hazel kneel down on all fours and crawl inside, her pale, marbled, muscleless buttocks shining at you with sickening unwelcome. She disappears inside.

Startled, you take a knee and see that she has slid away a wooden panel on the very bottom shelf and has entered into a tunnel of darkness. The only thing left of her is the snail trail of sticky ooze. Again, you follow.

Thirteen

The Tunnel

You pass the threshold of light and enter a brief moment of darkness before your eyes adjust. You are in a long, tight, very tight tunnel, so tight that your shoulders are smashed backward, and your head has to be turned slightly sideways in order to crawl, or more like slide, forward on your belly.

The tunnel isn't roughly hewn or dug out. It's clean, man-made, built with solid wood, and crafted with care and purpose.

You hear more than you see of Sister Hazel scraping down this wormhole. It's hot in here, and you start to sweat, but you can't wipe the beads from your forehead as they roll and burn your eyes. Blinking furiously, you crawl and pull your way through the hole and follow Hazel further inside.

The air is heavy and lacking. You do your best to shorten your breathing but the tugging, pulling, and crawling make it impossible. Before long, you feel the panic setting in; your brain fires up and tells your body that you need to turn the hell around and get out now.

A cold sweat and tremors saturate you as you actually contemplate your situation. However, you aren't able to look behind you; you can only guess that you are roughly 25 feet inside and totally fucked. Focusing forward, you can't see or hear Hazel anymore.

An image flashes inside your head:

It's your daughter around five years old, she has a backpack on, and she must be waiting to be picked up from school. A man walks up to her, and she runs into his arms with that smile that can cure any sickness. You see the man's face; it isn't you, it's someone else because you're missing, a corpse stuck in a secret tunnel of a house where nobody lives.

"Go!" you say aloud. You hate intrusive thoughts. You are aware of them, and by using anger, you can smash them into a tiny billion bits.

The tunnel ceiling has dropped even lower to the point where your head is completely turned to the right so that your cheek is rubbing the floor, but you continue forward like an inchworm.

You push your way forward while humming a song that doesn't exist. The humming helps you quicken up the pace.

Using the wiggling motion that your daughter uses when doing a happy dance, you manage to get further along and a few grinding minutes later, you see a pinprick of light up ahead. A smile creeps across your lips. Hope is a light, indeed.

The light is yellow and bright, most likely from an electrical source. This is good. But where are you? You crawled straight, which, if you think hard enough, means you went west. Which means you may be under what – the dining room, or the parlor, or maybe nowhere? Maybe you died already. Maybe this is a tunnel of the dead, and you are a ghoul stuck in a cycle of endless crawling, realizing, and starting over. But again, you focus on the light.

The light comes from a small crack in the wall in front of you. A closer examination shows that this isn't a wall, but rather another sliding panel. With the tips of your fingers, you slide the panel to the right, revealing a large opening.

Cold air rushes your face. You close your eyes, enjoying the gift even if the air itself is stale and sulfuric. This ecstasy is brief; you can't afford to waste time. You need to continue following Sister Hazel. Slowly, you inch over the edge and look down.

First, the opening is roughly 10ft x 10ft – it's very large. Secondly, the opening isn't a vast shaft that plummets into the sea of darkness below. Instead, a thin and crumbling staircase of stone winds down, down, down until it suddenly doesn't.

The first step is a good three-foot drop from where you lie. In order to get to it, you need to go hands and head first; you wouldn't be able to twist around in the tunnel and get your feet out first. The proposed task is insane because, unbeknownst to you, the width of the stairs is a mere two feet.

A fresh wave of panic sweeps you. Who the fuck made this insanity? It doesn't matter. It's here. You're here and stuck, you add, so you might as well figure this out.

Like a snail emerging from a breached shell, you slowly move forward. With great effort, you are able to get one arm out in front of you as the other grips the wooden edge as tight as possible. You stretch and reach out toward the bottom step as slowly as a caterpillar emerging from a chrysalis.

Your free hand is nearly there, but your stabilizing hand, the one gripping the edge of the shaft, needs adjusting. You can feel your hand slipping, so you decide to pause and anchor yourself so that you can slow your fall if it gets to that point.

Carefully and ever so slowly, you spread your legs and apply pressure to the tunnel walls. This braces you enough so that you can free your grip and drop down with ease. You land on the steps, stomach first.

After hugging the stairs for a moment, you slowly rise and take the pose of a surfer. Confident that you are not going to fall, you gradually start your descent.

It doesn't take long before you reach the first corkscrew turn; it's at this point that you look down and see Sister Hazel looking up at you from a few levels below. She points at you, mouth open, and then points at the bottom of the tunnel. She moves on, naked and hideous, mouth agape.

The situation makes you think about miners, specifically during the Neolithic age. How did they do it? Surely the first person or persons down must have died? So why keep it up? Maybe they used slaves. There might be a good story here, you think as you scrape ahead – the tragedy of a slave lost in a tunnel, with the only way out as digging deeper in.

You make a mental note to research ancient mining as your shoe kicks a pebble. The small crumb of stairs jumps a few steps before plummeting over the edge. The thought of Neolithic miners falls with it.

Your knee starts to ache like when you attempted to train for a marathon. If it wasn't for the random yet oddly timed series of sicknesses (hand, foot, and mouth, flu, cold, testicular infection), you would have probably been able to run the marathon. It didn't work out that way. That's life. Everything happens for a reason, you used to say; a kind of mantra that you picked up from your Grams, your adopted Grams, the one who loved you like a son.

But what about now? What about all this madness? What would Grams say now? Her voice fills your head, a high tone, a sweet voice that speaks plainly and always truthfully: "No good complaining about something you're already in. Figure it out and move on."

A slight dizziness hits you, but that doesn't really matter because you have finally reached the bottom turn. "Thank God," you say as you peer over the edge. What you see makes you jump a little, as if a small volt of electricity surged through you.

You see a boy chained to the floor by his ankle. The chain is heavy, like one of those chains you see on a boat – not a small boat, but a cruise ship. The boy is thin, dirty, and only wearing underwear. Standing over him is Sister Hazel. She looks at you and points to the boy.

"You see, I have you. You're right here. I never let you go. Do you see it now? I'll always have you," she says with the voice of a little girl.

The boy looks up at you, but his face is like a blurry photograph. It's impossible to recognize or even see human features. But it's clearly you, and most definitely you, right?

"What do you want from me?" you say, slowly walking down the last few steps with your hands up, showing her you mean no harm. Even though she doesn't project violence, something tells you to do it anyway.

"Stay with me." Her voice shifts into the man's now.

"I can't, Hazel. This isn't my home. You've always known that, haven't you?"

"Carver House is a House of God. It is a house for God's Children. You are a child of this house, and that means you are a child of God, and that means you are a part of this home, this house of God. Let me show you things." Her voice is now the normal 30-something-year-old voice that it should be.

"And what God is that, Hazel?"

Hazel laughs with her throat. She bends down and pulls the enormous chain free from the ground effortlessly. Using it like a leash, she leads the boy to the farthest wall of the cave-like room.

In the middle of the trickling wet wall, suspended without a frame, is a rounded wooden door painted brilliantly white.

Turning, Sister Hazel looks at you with her glowing white eyes, drooling mouth, erect penis, and dripping vagina.

"I've waited soooo long for this moment," she moans as she opens the door and disappears inside with the static-faced boy.

You follow not for her, not for you, but for him, the blurry-faced boy, because you begin to sense that you know something.

You enter the Cathedral:

The Cathedral has been carved inside the hollow earth with more beauty than Michelangelo could ever dream of. A million pews of marble disappear in endless rows. A long, carpeted aisle that cuts between the pews runs up to an altar which stands under a semi-dome of tiled mosaic pictures. On the altar is a long table full of food and drink – a feast.

Above you, a vaulted ceiling evaporates away because of the immensity of its depths. It's so immense it looks like a matte painting from an old movie. The walls are a riot of stained glass images and scenes that command all who witness them to stare in absolute awe.

What first you assumed were Christian images are actually scenes and images from your life: Babushka throwing a knife, you surrounded by darkness, Mother screaming at you, Mother burning cigarettes on you, Mother shoving fish down your throat, you being whipped by a vacuum cleaner cord, you on a bed with a man, a girl, a woman, and Cousin Richie. The images go on; some you don't understand or remember, and some you are positive aren't related to you. All are wretched.

"Welcome to your Cathedral," Sister Hazel says, walking down the aisle with the boy towards the feast under the dome. She says this without turning around.

"I built this for you," she continues. "We started this the day they took you away from us. It's my design, though. I poured all of my passion for you into it. Each stone, each piece of glass, every inch of this cathedral has you inside it."

"I don't understand..." you say, dumbfounded as you reach her. Your eyes are still looking around at the vast impossibleness of it all.

"You don't need to understand," she sings while sitting on a chair made of living people. "You aren't meant to understand things that happen to you. What matters is that you are here to give a face, to give reason to all of this, all of this that is yours, all of this that you left behind."

You stare at the vile chair and shudder at the nameless faces and sexless bodies. You tear your eyes away and look around, and somewhere in the cathedral or in your head, the dark monastery chants of Monasterium Imperi start to play.

The living chair of human body parts crawls like a hand toward you. You don't have time to react as it forces you to sit on it. It's warm and moist.

Hands, where the armrests should be, grab you tight and hold you firm as the rest of the damnation scurries back to the feast of a giant turkey, steaming piles of potatoes, roasted pork, endless mountains of colorful fruit, a pond of borscht, a pyramid of cakes, and a bucket of wine.

You test the strength of the chair but give up because it has you down good. You feel something wet on your ankle and look down to see a tongue licking you. You jerk your leg away. The tongue slips back to wherever it came from.

The insanity of this world is too real for you to even begin to challenge its legitimacy. To argue such a thing would prove to be pointless. The fact is that this is the reality that you are stuck in.

"The boy...is that me?" you question, tilting your head from right to left in hopes of seeing past the fuzziness of the boy's face.

"Yes," says Hazel, who stares at you while her hand gently rests on the boy's naked knobby knee. The hand slowly walks towards the place it should never go.

"Don't touch him!" you roar, trying to stand up.

Sister Hazel smiles, "I already have, remember?"

She stands up and walks to you. Kneeling down, she looks you in the eyes.

You look away as if the very sight of her burns you, but you can't really avoid her because dancing fingers erupt from the chair and hold your head still.

In her eyes, you see the faces of everyone you ever met inside the Carver House. You see every memory of pain and suffering. Her eyes are a conduit of all the wrong things. You start to feel full as she continues to bore into you.

"A feast of memory is it not?" she says while licking her lips and rubbing your leg. "You will never leave me again, and in time, I will stain your living seed."

The living chair starts to tremble and shake as you struggle fiercely. Boiling tears of rage consume you beyond anything you have ever felt.

The face of your daughter; the joy of her birth; the passion behind her conception; the cross above the hospital bed; the guardian angel pin; more intrusive thoughts of all the awful things that might happen to your daughter slowly conquer your mind.

Madness, the man, begins to form in your mind. You need to take control of this situation now!

You close your eyes and slow down your breathing. You start to visualize something – an endless library. The one you created as a child. This makes you smile, but the smile is quickly stolen because you can feel an unwanted presence behind you – the lurking fear of the past, present, and future.

You need to survive, so you enter the library of your mind.

***

Inside you do not see endless bookshelves, rather you see a library catalog cabinet that reaches to the sky. With great haste, you walk to the center of the cabinet and pull open drawer 178 to find hundreds of memory cards.

Your mind cycles through selected memories like a Rolodex. It's slow because the modality behind the Rolodex is tedious, but precise. It is effective because each memory card in your head contains a Dewey

Decimal number that is organized in the classic Dewey Decimal System way. The methodology is accurate and efficient.

The card you find is numbered the way you remember it: 11122019. With a thumb and forefinger, you extract it, put it before your mind's eye, and take it in forever. The memory has been checked out: Birth of Your Daughter - 11122019 EHH EH EVENING Girl, 12 LBS, 21 Inches.

Fourteen

Now you are free of those unwanted thoughts, those rotten memories; you are renewed with the reminder of the importance of your life, and that is to make sure your daughter, the new life, does not suffer the way you did. It'll be hard, but all you need to do is focus on the card. #11122019 EHH EH.

"You'll be okay," says a voice from behind you.

You turn and see yourself, but not in a way you fully recognize. This version of you is flawless, as though you'd never walked the earth, never carried a cross, and were simply a being sent from God himself.

"You need only to believe in yourself. Remember what Blessed Mother Sarah Connor said – no fate but what we make."

You nod your head at the brilliance of yourself, this icon of hope and logic. You feel like a man who understands fate.

***

You return from your mind as if only a blink of a moment had passed to see that Sister Hazel is standing by the table now. She's looking up dramatically.

"Descend, Mommy!"

The ceiling opens up and a huge flesh crane, dripping wet, lowers from an opening of the dome.

The claw of the crane holds the bloated monster whale, Mother, who wears a silk nightgown and little white shoes. She sings some sort of opera that makes you fall over in your chair, but the chair rights you quickly.

The crane reaches the table and releases Mother, who stumbles on her feet and straightens up with a proud shake.

The smell of Mother and the crane's mucus makes you recoil in disgust. It smells like phlegm from a bad sinus infection and stale beer. You watch the crane as it ascends back up and notice that its flesh is wet because it's sweating.

"What a feast," loudly moans Mother as she poofs down on one of the chairs. Her weight makes the chair shake, but it holds firm. Mother, without acknowledging you or anything else, begins to gorge with her bare hands.

The chair releases you, and you stand up. You watch as Sister Hazel skittles over to Mother, pulls down Mother's silken top, and out falls a massive breast full of green veins. Hazel begins to suckle from the mouthful of nipple. Mother moans while chewing.

"Yessssss, eat my love, drink my love, yesssss."

Without hesitation, you move to the boy and free him from his shackles. You pull him to his feet, but he resists.

"Come on, damn it!"

"No," says the boy.

You look at him, and his face clears. His face is your childhood face: blue eyes, buzz-cut hair, and a dirty but always caring expression, edged with a sense of understanding and experience he shouldn't have.

"I can't go with you, but you can go alone," he says.

"You have to. You don't understand what they'll do to you, please!" you sob.

The pain is real. The reality of what has happened and what will happen is as sharp as a piano note, as real as the words you read. It's the utmost factual reality that all who are suffering must face. The feeling of knowing something grows deeper inside you.

"It's going to be okay," says the boy with a smile as he gently holds your hand.

"No, it won't," you say through streams of tears – tears that you suppressed since childhood.

The boy tugs your hand until you are kneeling in front of him. With both of his hands, he holds your face so that you look at him, really look at him. It's at this point that you feel a warm sensation run through your very core. A pleasant, safe feeling that is reserved for sacred things like fine music, beautiful poetry, or reviving literature.

"You are loved," says the boy as he holds your head to his chest. "This house of wood and stone is not a house of God – we are."

His words amplify like an electric pulse that surrounds you like a shield. You look up at him and understand everything, but because you understand, you are also afraid. You tell him.

"I'm afraid."

"Why?"

"I'm afraid to be alone."

"Even Jesus was alone."

You stare at the boy, who is you, and nod. The missing truth, the lost answer, the deepest thorn, has finally been answered, found, plucked. The great purging has given you a clear vision of the arcane depths of lost time, of suppressed memory.

Now, in the waking clarity of eyes, you must seek out the opalescent ending that you need. It's the elixir of suffering, the antidote of sorrow, the cure for the poison that this house released inside you; the slow poison that rotted your very soul. A poison that you now believe to be genetic and inherited. You can feel it, the poison stirring inside you because your white blood cells, the ones that are neon-charged, are fighting back with ferocity.

"It's the only way to stop the cycle," whispers the boy.

Is he reading my mind? you think, but remember that your minds are one and the same. Nodding, you dig inside your pocket and give the boy the rosary that Father Dan gave you. The boy cups it in his hands as if holding the sacred Marian promises himself.

A tremendous warmth pulls you to the boy. You hug, and the warmth becomes something like light itself until it envelops and melts you together like light embracing shadow.

Ignoring the feasting of Mother and the great sucking from Sister Hazel, you get up and walk over to one of the brass candelabras on the table. The candelabra is dense in your hand as you pick it up, first with one hand but quickly with two, because it is heavier than it should be in your small hands.

"What are you doing, boy?" says Mother as she drinks from the gravy train.

Your lips move, but nothing is said because it doesn't matter what you say. What you are doing is what you want to do, and what you want to do is solely yours and yours alone. Smiling, you raise the candelabra over your head and throw it at Mother.

Instantly, the flames erupt when they touch her sweating, oily skin. It's as if her sweat is combustible. The flames jump onto Sister Hazel. They both continue to eat and suck without any resistance or reaction. It doesn't take long for the table, the floor, and the walls to catch. Suddenly, as if turning a page, the cathedral is an inferno.

Time to run.

You turn, but the door you came from is behind a wall of flame that is slowly eating its way to you.

"Help!" you yell at the man who is bathing in the fire with pleasure.

"The mirror, go to the mirror," he says, pointing up at the now-lowering crane above.

"I think we can both leave," you say, looking at the descending crane and back at the man.

"No fate but what we make," says the man as he slowly ashes away like pages of a burning book.

You give him a second of prayer, or something close to it, before you jump up and grab the crane. The tight skin of the machine is slippery in your small hands, but you hold on as it grinds and groans loudly up, up, up.

Before you reach the top, you look down and see the flaming versions of Mother, Sister Hazel, and somehow now Cousin Richie, looking up at you.

They're holding hands, and tears of charcoal slide down their melted faces like mud. You cough up a snot bomb and spit as the crane jolts to a stop.

Looking up, you see a paneled door and question how Mother could fit through it before you push it open and find yourself inside a foggy and syrupy mirror world.

Hoisting yourself up, you find that your movements are slow, but you can move freely. The only thing on your mind is getting out as you look around.

On the wall behind you is the other side of the mirror. It's as bright, clear, and wide as a 75-inch 4k LED television. Moving towards it as quickly as possible, you eagerly peer inside and jump back.

Staring back at you is a woman holding a baby girl to her hip. She looks confused and afraid as she sees you.

Slowly, she comes closer to the mirror. Her trembling hand touches the mirror surface but is quickly pulled back. The little girl on her hip giggles and kicks.

"What are you doing in there?"

"I really can't explain it," you say exhaustedly.

She furrows her brow, and you think you see a bit of sadness cross her eyes.

"Who are you?" the woman questions.

"I think you know."

"But...I don't understand?"

"I know you don't, but I really can't explain it."

"Where is he? Tell me where my–"

"I can't do that."

"And why is that?!" she says tersely.

"I can't feel it, my memory. It's fading. It's like words falling off a page, if such a thing could happen. I don't understand it. Everything, all of me, is getting scattered. I had to start over. We agreed that this was the only way."

"The only way what? What is this?" she says frantically.

You look at her daughter, who is looking at you, or at your reflection. You aren't sure, and you don't want to be sure because the sight of her makes your heart explode into a million pieces. You let it blow because of the poison of this place and the promise you made to yourself.

"The house, the Carver House, is not sustainable. It poisoned me, and that same poison will poison her."

The woman looks at her daughter and back at you. "What poison? What do you mean? Who are you really?"

"I can't protect her. I can't keep her safe when she grows up. The world, our world, it's all poisoned. The roots of this house have spread too far. Whatever I do, whatever planning I put forth won't be enough, do you understand? She's the future of all of us, and she's already doomed to suffer. I can't watch her go through that. It's like waiting for the worst thing that you know will happen, just not when it will happen or how it will happen. I don't want her to live my fate."

"What fate!?" she screams.

You look at her and speak:

"When I was a child..."

You speak words never told to anybody. Not even God. But now, in your reflection, in your arms, you cry. And your reflection, the young boy, not the man, does the same.

You weep, and she weeps. You pray. She prays. You are a mirror. This is the truth – an immortal reflection that is finally seen. A reality finally realized.

The woman sees you, the boy and the man, for the first time. You know now that she understands everything because you are both crying the same type of lipid, water and mucus.

With each story and memory that is extracted from the deepest well that you hold, the truth floods out like sweet salvation. You cannot contain it, so your dam bursts forth, and for a long while, it rushes and gushes until it only drips and drips. It is done. You have lived, and you are now living again.

The image of the woman and her daughter ripples and spreads like a quiet lake disturbed by a stone. Eventually, the ripples spread and do not stop. They begin to take the form of neon electrical signals that pulse and spread and repeat over and over again.

You watch as the woman and the child begin to vanish, not into a painful nothingness but into a salvation that you have created for them. They are stored in a million neurons that have been charged by this neon wave. The mirror begins to melt.

"What's happening?" she whimpers as she hugs her daughter.

"I'm saving her."

You stand there, still in your underwear, and watch the mirror bubble, boil, and slide down the wall like magma down a hill. It rolls and flows slowly until it has completely changed its molecular structure.

Taking a breath; you are breathing. Something overcomes you, a great wave of nostalgia for something you can't quite remember because time is being fast-forwarded like a VHS tape.

The feeling and the momentary relapse of memory are pushed away because the floor you stand on begins to smoke and become hot – the fire below has found you.

The house shakes, and the floor begins to buckle. You take off running just as a symphony of flames burst through the floor. As you jump over the sofa, you look back and swear that the fire is moving in the shape of people. No time to fear this as you race down the hallway, past the bathroom, and straight into the foyer.

This part of the house is also on fire. The grand staircase is an avalanche of rolling flames, but those chairs that nobody sits on are left untouched. With you is a galaxy of moths, all shimmering chitin that look like mad little blinks of light.

Enough of this scene; you race to the front door, and just as you are about to grab it, a voice from the hallway calls out to you. But you are free of any more Carver House hauntings, so you grab the double doors and pull them open with tremendous force.

You fall out and down the steps and onto the gravel and grass. You lie there on your back, looking up at the strong blue sky laced with white stratus clouds.

You smile and laugh because you feel free, but you are not completely sure why. You turn your head towards the town, and you see flashing lights rushing towards you. Still smiling, you turn your head back to the house and watch it burn.

As the flames rage and burst out the window, you slowly feel a pleasant sensation cover you once again, but the roaring of the oncoming sirens softly brings you back to the burning of Carver House.

Sitting up, you stare transfixed at the top floor and watch as Mother's room collapses.

Fifteen

Deep inside the inferno, you can hear the house screaming.

Sixteen

You find a slice of silence and a bit of sleep as the fire turns to cinders and the smoke settles. The days and nights inside the Carver House are untraceable. You are nothing but a boy, naked, lying in the grass, kissed by the autumn dew.

Did the old priest come first, or was he already waiting? He picks you up and wraps you in a dusty gray blanket that itches your skin. He whispers the Hail Mary, and you sleep like a child.

***

The hours of questions from the priest who calls himself Father Dan fog your young mind. You can barely see mere silhouettes, so you do not know where you are, but it smells of lavender, rose, and frankincense.

Father Dan – Boy, where is the man that went into the house?

You – I am the only one.

Father Dan – And where is your mother? Where is your sister, huh?

You – I have no mother. I have no sister.

Father Dan – Who are you? What do you remember?

You – Leave me alone, Priest.

Father Dan – ...Pray for us sinners now, and at the hour of our death, amen.

You (sleeping again) – I am not dead but born again...

***

You wake up and find yourself in a hotel room wearing sweatpants and a matching sweater that belongs to a local middle school. Father Dan is watching you. The hotel bed you lie on is exquisite and offered you no dreams or, better yet, no nightmares.

The cooing of mourning doves outside your window gives you life and you instantly feel it – the radical change of your constitution.

Sitting up, your mind wanders, and you can't recall what yesterday held, or any other day before that. Not even the smoke you wear triggers a memory. For this you are grateful, but you do not know why.

Again, you sleep.

***

A knock on the door a day later wakes you, and the voice of a young lady reminds you about checkout time. Father Dan complies and commands you to gather your things, the few that they are, and pack.

You desire to brush your teeth and wash your face with the small sample-sized toiletries in the bathroom that you know are waiting for you. As you scrub, brush, and rinse, you feel the sudden urge to go home. This feeling intensifies as you question your youthful face. You see the face of a boy, age ten, through the eyes of a dreaming man, but you do not know what it means.

Exiting the bathroom, face not fully dry, you turn to leave but stop. An autumn breeze from the window left ajar says something to you in a language long forgotten. A feeling of nostalgia from a long, distant memory.

Shouldering your bag, you walk to the desk that sits bolted under the window. The desk contains a single pull out drawer. You open it and see a black copy of the King James Bible. Turning your head, you see that Father Dan is outside in the hallway with his back to you. Quickly, you take the bible and put it in your bag. Muttering an apology to the air, you exit the room to join Father Dan.

After a significant breakfast, you get into Father Dan's car. The gray curtain of autumn is endless, but it is not gloomy. Instead, you find it comforting as Father Dan drives without music.

You – Where are we going?

Father Dan – Do not ask questions that you already know the answers to.

Turning your head, you watch the scenery pass by like faded brushstrokes. You do not have any real thoughts besides getting...

You – ...Home?

Father Dan – Yes.

***

As the miles turn over, you begin to remember a feeling. It feels like you know where you put something but cannot find it, not really, because you can't really lose things that aren't yours.

Father Dan takes a right inside a large apartment building parking lot full of cars. He manages to find a spot near a walking bridge that covers the small brook that feeds a pond.

Turning off the car, he turns to you with great sadness and hands you a pair of charred black keys and a melted ID.

Father Dan – Delight yourself in the Lord, and he will give you the desires of your heart.

A sense of urgency consumes you. You grab the key but leave the ID and quickly exit the car, speed walk to the front door, fumble with your key, enter the building, and hop up the stairs two at a time, somehow knowing where to go. You are excited, and not sure why. The memories stretch in front of you like a ripple.

You enter the hallway of the fourth floor and see apartment 4B, the one with the Halloween wreath, appear. It makes you smile.

You finger the apartment key and insert it into the top lock. The sound of the deadbolt scraping along the crooked strike plate and the woosh of the door opening finds you inside the apartment at last.

As you kick off your shoes and place your bag on the floor next to the hallway closet with the full-length mirror, a familiar feeling of expectation hits you. It flutters like a moth in your stomach as you enter the empty kitchen and look around.

This feeling gives you great pause because it is truly physical. It's like a bubble rising yet not bursting, a sort of endless anticipation that is never released. Taking these thoughts and feelings, you walk throughout the apartment, searching for something.

From the kitchen, you enter the dining room area and find the table empty. Then you turn and look at the living room, which is empty as if not lived in at all.

Pursing your lips, you rub your stomach and walk to your bedroom, where you find it sparse and only containing a large bed.

You sit on the bed and breathe in the regular old silence that lives inside all family-deprived apartments. This is normal, you think, but the moths inside your stomach are multiplying. This is fine, you think, but the moths inside are raging.

You stand up because they tell you to. As you do, your socked foot crunches something on the ground. Looking down, you see that you are standing on a picture frame.

Removing your foot, you bend down, pick up the frame, and turn it over so that you can see what it contains.

The image is of a woman holding a child, a girl no more than six months old. They smile at you. Their smiles aren't casual, but rather ones given to someone who is truly seen, who is truly loved. The moths are screaming now.

A cold sweat covers your body as your hands tremble. You stare at the photo, at the woman, at the child, but you do not know who they are. This frustrates you, like a fleeting thought or memory struggling to surface – one you once buried to move on.

You smell rotted wood, smoke-drenched cloth, hot sulfur, morning coffee, sauce-drenched eggs, spicy chorizo, and you feel the gentle tug of tiny hands on yours, the light little lips of good night kisses upon your cheek, the tight squeeze of arms around your neck. And then you remember the promise that you couldn't keep, and the metamorphosis that you conjured up like some sort of pagan mystic that forgot the begotten son and the immortal promise.

You fall to your knees and feel the universe inside you collapsing because of something that you did, yet have no real memory of.

The pain is cosmic as it surges through you like ten thousand volts of ethereal electricity that supercharges everything that you have inside, but not the thing you need to remember.

A voice sounds behind you. It's Father Dan, and he looks at you with pity and contempt.

"You, the thing who emerged from the fires below, will live in anguish but not understand why."

"The thing below? If I am not the man, who am I?" you ask.

"You are nothing. You mean nothing. I am afraid, boy, that you are no child of God. Not anymore. Not without your suffering."

"What happens now?"

"You must find suffering. You will go back and rebuild the house of God again."

"Again?"

"I am afraid you have done this before, boy."

Obsidian weariness, regret, and the desire to hold someone fall upon you like a thick blanket of utter despair and sorrow. You find no comfort in the face of the priest.

You weep.

Authors Note

Thank you to everyone who has sailed with me over the years. A special thanks to my writing partner and champion—Jay, our late-night writing sessions have shaped me in more ways than I can count. I look forward to the next one.

About the Author

Eric David Ami is a writer whose work explores the intersection of faith, fear, and the unknown. Born in Chicago, Illinois, he studied film before working numerous odd jobs, including working on the remake of A Nightmare on Elm Street, construction, and as a private security officer. A former foster kid, he brings a distinct perspective shaped by resilience, displacement, and the search for belonging—threads that often surface in his storytelling.

When not writing fiction, he discusses and writes about pop culture.

House of God marks his debut in fiction.

Meet the Artist

Bryan Christopher Moss is a Grammy-nominated visionary artist celebrated for his fusion of traditional fine arts with contemporary styles. Known for his vibrant color palettes and meticulous detail, he explores themes of identity, cultural heritage, and the human experience, often drawing inspiration from nature and urban life. His work spans various media, including painting, sculpture, and comics, where he marries expressive brushwork with narrative storytelling to evoke raw emotion and introspection. You can find him online @strangethingsmoss or at bryanmossart.com.